# White Trash Warm Hearts

## A Steel Magnolia's Journey from Tears to Triumph

Judy H James

**BALBOA**
PRESS

A DIVISION OF HAY HOUSE

Balboa Press books may be ordered through booksellers or by contacting:

Balboa Press
A Division of Hay House
1663 Liberty Drive
Bloomington, IN 47403
www.balboapress.com
1 (877) 407-4847

Print information available on the last page.

ISBN: 978-1-9822-2304-5 (sc)
ISBN: 978-1-9822-2305-2 (e)

Balboa Press rev. date: 03/08/2019

# DEDICATION

This book is dedicated to my many Teachers:

My children, each a genius:
Rob, Scott, Bo, Abby, and Jody;
and their father Jerry.

My friend who taught us all so much,
Luiz da Silva;

My spiritual teachers:
Rev. Elizabeth Claire and
Rev. Ken Wilcox

My first teacher, my mother,
Florence Devine Hughey.

Each of you have contributed
so very much to my life!
Thank you!

# Table of Contents

# Steel Magnolia

I'm a Southern belle
Through and through
I'm tough as nails
And genteel too
I may sound funny
And
My name's Judy Sue
But watch out
I may fool you.

# My Family's Journey – 1931 to 1960

1931: Hal Holt Sisk- legally changed to Hughey is born in Shelby, NC

1936: Iris is born in Spartanburg, SC

1938: Judy is born in Rutherfordton, NC, at aunt's home

1939: World War II starts in Europe, ends in 1945

1940: Max is born in Ruth, NC

1941: Family in Spartanburg, SC (U.S. enters WWII in December)

1942: Becky is born in Spindale, NC; then family is in Shelby, NC, with various maternal aunts

1943: Family in Shelby, NC; leaves for Patterson, NJ; moves on to Virginia

1944: Coastal Virginia for family– Judy in Bridgewater, VA

1946: Judy returns to family at Woody Park, VA

1947: Family: Time in Norfolk, VA; returns to Woody Park, VA

1949: Judy only: Virginia, to Baltimore, MD; on to Gilkey, NC; then to Patterson, NC, and Shelby, NC; to Union Mills, NC. Family: various places in NC.

1949 to 1951: the orphanage in Union Mills, NC -the four siblings.

1951: March- murder in Union Mills, NC, then in Dec. '51, Judy and family move to Spindale, NC

1952: Iris marries, goes to San Diego; family in Spindale, NC

1952 – September 1952-56: NC - Judy's high school days in Spindale, NC

1956 - 1958:

> Judy at Gardner Webb College; family in Spindale, NC – Judy works summer job in Atlanta, GA.; My 2nd Summer: Shelby, NC

1958-1960:

Wake Forest University, Winston Salem, NC

1960: Judy graduates, marries, moves to St. Petersburg, Florida

# Definition of Terms

**cold grits:** In my story this term refers to hard times, meaning when all that is left to eat is cold, leftover grits, or maybe less than that.

**steel magnolia:** Southerners know what this means, but for the rest of y'all, it's a term for Southern women who may seem frail, but they are able to survive the most difficult times through their own wits, steely determination and more natural common sense than anyone has a right to possess. Scarlet O'Hara, in *Gone with the Wind*, is the ideal example of this. Know this, though: There is always drama when a steel magnolia is in residence and although life is interesting, it's not always completely safe. The magnolia is not as beautiful as some flowers, yet it is a symbol of strength and is naturally attractive. The "steel magnolia" is always fascinating, unpredictable and yes, often a little on the crazy side.

**warm hearts:** Y'all know, of course, that this stands for the close family ties that help us survive, which really were our salvation in childhood.

**white trash:** The lowest rung on the social ladder for whites in the South.

**y'all:** This is truly a handy little term that means "all of you," and I've always felt that anyone with good sense would adopt it. It really does come in handy since it includes everyone—or can be confusing when you want it to be, as to who it does include.

# My Story—

# Believe

# It or Not

I come from a long line of steel magnolias.

This is my story as a child of the South, living in poverty and confusion, and my journey as I searched for the good life. At a very young age I wanted to get an education to escape poverty, and to find out what a normal life really felt like. I truly yearned to move out of the 'white trash' class of the South and become something more; but it did seem almost impossible. People seemed to be sending me a clear message: "Born in poverty, die in poverty." This was especially true for girls and, as my aunt told me, "Honey, you need education like you need a hole in the head, 'cause in the end you're jus' goin' to marry and have babies." Everything in me rebelled against this, so I was both molded and motivated by poverty and these Southern beliefs. Despite these ever-present influences, I never allowed them to control me.

I come from a long line of steel magnolias, which means we can survive almost anything. I'm proud to be called one since there was a lot of surviving going on in my childhood. I needed all the courage and moxie I could muster up. We often had cold grits, or not even that to eat at times, yet we did have Momma's love. I was also determined to get an education to help Momma have a more secure, happy life, and my siblings wanted to assist her as well. We were often separated from Momma, with each of us in different relatives' homes or in much less acceptable places. We knew, however, that Momma would come for us as soon as she could. Daddy was a different matter, though; he was not around most of the time, especially when we needed him.

I am a true Southerner, and everyone knows this immediately when they hear my accent, which they claim to love. I've always had my doubts about that. When I was president of the chamber of commerce in a Florida county, we were hosting several travel agents from Japan. I was talking with a group when one Japanese lady who was listening very carefully, suddenly said to me, "We just visited Nashville and met several country singers, are you related to Dolly Parton?" I confessed I was not related to Dolly but would be proud if I were. Afterwards, my friends and I had a great laugh. I was told by a new friend, a Harvard graduate from Boston: "Honestly, Judy, until I got to know you, I thought that anyone who talks like you was ignorant and uneducated." That stung, so I wrote her my poem, "Steel Magnolia," which she liked, and it suggests we Southerners may fool you. Many people still hold those beliefs about Southerners, though, and it's always fun to surprise them.

During my childhood, I lived in many towns and cities in the South, but I never for a moment took on all the beliefs of those who surrounded me. We lived in Patterson, New Jersey, and Baltimore for short periods too, but we definitely were misfits that far up North. As a child, I lived in North Carolina and Virginia and as an adult I've lived in many Southern towns including several in Florida, so like it or not I am soaked in Southernerness. I am very much like the Scotch-Irish clan which produced me. There are things that I love and respect about the South; however, other things I don't care for, such as the rigid social structure for many people here, especially African Americans. Had I been around during the Civil War, I would have supported Lincoln and the Union (but not Sherman's destructive march through the South) which of course is complete heresy for many Southerners. Honestly, I do sometimes think God made a rare mistake and dropped me down into the wrong family and the wrong region. I'm sure there have been many times when my brothers and sisters would shout, "Amen!" to that. But we all know God does not make mistakes.

Many Southern writers have found much to write about in this region. Mark Twain penned wonderful tales dealing with its good and bad traits and he too had a deep connection to it. I believe that no matter how far away we go, we'll return to the South eventually, like my brother Max did, even after having experienced the world. The South has an interesting history, a slow, friendly pace, the gorgeous Blue Ridge Mountains, numerous weird oddities and many lovely normal people too. All of this calls us back into the area's soft, sweet, crazy life.

In my efforts to overcome the confusion and instability of my childhood, I've had to do a lot of digging to let go of the garbage (hate, resentment, anger, and so on) which I latched on to as a child and which became a part of me as an adult. I have no need to blame anyone else because I know now that everyone did the best they could. The purpose in my journey has been to know what true abundance is, to learn to love myself and others and then to find peace and joy in life. I've always wanted to dance to my own unique tune and assist others in doing the same, especially children.

I went to six schools during the sixth grade and had already skipped the second and third grades because of illness. I lived in more than twenty places before I finished college and our moves were not for pleasure but out of true necessity. Momma had a difficult time supporting us alone, so we moved many times in search of the good life, which eluded us for much too long. I dreamed of a better life and Momma convinced me it would come through education, which she preached about constantly. Momma repeatedly told me, "You really can better yourself, if you want to bad enough." I believed her. I borrowed money and worked my way through college. After I quit working at about age thirty, I enjoyed many years as a volunteer and a child advocate in Florida.

With the exception of a short time, I have lived in Florida since 1960. I now live in St. Augustine; I find the town totally fascinating and never tire of its wonders. I love its history, unique architecture, artsy flavor and the fact that it is surely haunted. After all, five bloody flags have flown over our mighty fort, the Castillo de San Marcos. Many were killed here: the Seminoles, British, French, Spanish, Confederates and, finally, the Americans who each decided at various times that they coveted this lovely place by the sea. They fought, killed burned and captured it several times over. St. Augustine became a town back in 1565, under the Spanish, and is the oldest city in the United States. There are probably spirits swirling all around us and the locals swear they can feel the ghosts of the many warriors and settlers who have died here—but that's another story.

At about 62 years old, I decided I wanted to transform my life and I was sincere in wanting to improve. Many years after that decision, I am now a more spiritual and perhaps a better person. My sisters Iris and Becky, who are steel magnolias in their own right, and I disagree on religion, yet I know they are good Christians. I have faith we'll all meet in that heavenly place with my brother Max, Momma, Daddy and my other five half-siblings. Quite possibly, we will also run into both of my unpleasant grandmothers, who are probably still feuding on the other side. Seeing me there will be a shock for my sisters, who are absolutely certain that Saint Peter will never allow me to step one foot through that heavenly gate. I often ask them, "Is heaven really a gated community?" They are positive that it is and that gate will not open for me; nor will I become a resident of the city with the golden streets.

It might help the reader to know a little bit about my rather interesting grouping of siblings. Momma married and had one child (Hal), then divorced, married my daddy, who already had one son (Jim), and they had the four of us who were raised by Momma: Iris, me, Max and Becky. Then after they divorced, Daddy married again and had three more children. If my odd set of siblings is too confusing, don't bother with this. I don't want to muddy the waters of a story which is already pretty murky. There were nine of us in all, but because of Daddy's wayward life there may be others who we have not discovered yet.

My siblings will not see our story as I do. For that reason, I hope each one writes about their life, which was as unstable and odd as mine. One thing we all remember well, however, is the double murder and its impact on our lives. The murders were not in the family, but they were much too close. It could be helpful if each sibling writes a book about our life, which was so mobile that we lost track of people, dates and many facets of our childhood. What little we owned including the family photos were destroyed in a fire, which we suspect was insurance-connected arson when we left Baltimore in 1949. As a result, we did not even have family photos and mementoes to help us piece together our wandering life. What I have, I've begged, borrowed and taken from relatives.

Momma would not talk about the past; she said she'd rather forget most of it, seeing no value in remembering painful memories. Amazingly, despite our life of mobility and weirdness, we are all rather successful in various ways. We rarely agree, however, on anything religious, political or the state of the union. You might ask what we talk about. We manage, although at times it does get rather spirited. We laugh often and recall some of the crazy times in our childhood, such as the trip down South, from Baltimore, in 1949. Nine of us crammed into my cousin's car which could hold only four or five comfortably. We stopped many times in order that those of us stuffed into the trunk could be switched out, so no one suffocated in there.

Somewhere along the way, I decided my childhood had been interesting and challenging enough that it might be worth telling. After all, I survived and in the end I thrived through the journey. I know that everything which happens to us and the choices we make mold us into who we become as adults. I have no regrets; I now see my rambling childhood as an interesting story chocked-full of lessons and fashioned just for me. They say you can't change your childhood, but you can change the way you feel about it.

So, I have set about doing that and writing my story is a big part of my emotional journey. I've written this book to confront my childhood and it has sometimes been difficult. In the end, I can say it's been a wonderful experience. I want my children, grandchildren and especially my two great grandchildren, handsome Dolton and lovely Callan and those of future generations to understand my journey, their family and past generations. I'd like them to know what helped me to accomplish what I wanted in life. I once heard someone say, "If you want something, paint your desire with very colorful emotions on the canvas of your heart, and it will come into your life." I'd like to inspire children to believe that you can have anything you really want, but with a warning: "Be careful what you ask for, because you'll probably get it."

I know that love is the gentlest and yet the most powerful force on earth and the only thing in life that is truly important. I hope reading about my journey brings a few lessons, maybe a few tears and a lot of laughs, because in the end it was the love and laughter that saved my family as we survived life in our beloved South.

I call this book my journey; some might call it simply a story; but some in my family may want to call it just a whole lotta lies. My book has been about seventy years in incubation, so now that it has finally hatched, some may detect a few deformities (or mistakes) in it. For this, I beg forgiveness because most of it is based on the memories of a child. Nevertheless, here is my wandering, crazy, interesting life as I remember it. Y'all can believe it or not, yet I do hope you will enjoy it.

Please note that I have written each chapter in this book to stand alone. Therefore, some facts might be repeated.

# A Gift

There is no past
It is truly only what
You now perceive it to be
And there is no future
It is only what you
Might now envision it to be.
There is forever, only Now
Your Present
A gift to you
And Now is everything
Wonderful
That you choose it to be.

# Grandma, the Mighty Steel Magnolia

My aunts threw everything we owned onto a sheet in the yard. I can still feel the shame of seeing that white ball with our clothes in it. However, there was worse to follow.

I hated my grandma until the day she died because she treated my Momma absolutely terrible for her entire life. For many years I felt completely justified in my hatred of her. Grandma Cora Akers Devine was many things—some good and some anything but good. She was charming, spiteful, loving, cold, smart, superstitious and unbelievably powerful. Although she was a small, thin woman, she had total control of our large Southern clan as the grand matriarch, and how she judged you pretty well determined whether you were happy or miserable in the family. She was a steel magnolia of the first order, meaning a strong and demanding "drama queen" who held court every day. She loved and spoiled her favorites but made life almost unbearable for many. I witnessed her awful treatment of my Momma many times and as a child I thought this unforgivable.

My worst memory was when I was about four years old and Becky was a baby in Momma's arms. Momma had decided to go back to Daddy again because she couldn't work at that time, after her accident in the cotton mill. Grandma, who hated my daddy, pitched a terrifying hissy fit. Actually, she had good reason for her hatred of Daddy, but more than anything she hated losing control or not getting her way. So when Momma told her she felt she had to go with Daddy to New Jersey over her objections, Grandma demanded that my three aunts with whom we were living in Shelby, North Carolina, throw us out of their various homes immediately. As always, they obeyed her without a word. Grandma had lost control of a daughter and although Momma was not one of her favorites, Grandma was furious.

They threw our clothes onto a sheet in my aunt's yard, and I can still feel the embarrassment of seeing that sheet tied into a big white ball, with our meager belongings in it. However, the worst was yet to come. It seemed to me that the whole world was watching as Grandma then slapped Momma in the face and screamed, "You're nothing but a whore. I never want to see you again and don't you ever come back here." God, how I wanted to cry! But I knew the last thing my Momma needed was a crybaby on her hands, so I swallowed my tears along with the pain in my chest. After cutting her deeply with those awful words, Grandma then twisted the knife deeper into the heart by telling Momma, "I'm keeping Hal and if you dare to try to take him from me, I'll ruin you. I'll bring the welfare down on your head and have 'em take away all your kids." No one doubted for a moment that she would bring 'the hounds of hell' down on Momma and that she could get the family to back her.

She kept my half-brother for the rest of his life, as if she had the divine right to do so. Momma was so frightened Grandma would carry out her threat that she never even tried to get Hal. He never understood why he couldn't live with us and it had a terrible effect on him. Although he was very bright, was charming, an amazing baseball player and loved his children a great deal, he died much too young. When he was a child, he begged to stay with us and we all wanted him to, and we didn't understand why he couldn't live with us. Momma never explained to us or to Hal about the threat Grandma held over her head. I had forgotten about it because that whole terrible event was much too painful to remember.

This is how we left the bosom of Momma's family—in the midst of tremendous pain, spitefulness and what felt like pure hatred to me. We would not return for about eight years, which were difficult times, especially for Momma. I was twelve years old and was in an orphanage when Grandma died. I celebrated openly and, without any shame, declared, "Good riddance to bad rubbish because we'll all be happier without her." This shocked my sister, Iris, who loved Grandma with all her heart since she'd been one of her favorites. Grandma Devine, however, was not the sweet grandmother in the kitchen baking us goodies; rather, it was mostly dark drama which she cooked up in our lives. Making matters worse, as usual Grandma turned out to be right about Daddy. He dumped us as soon as possible.

Grandma had eleven children, many grandchildren, great-grandchildren and in-laws; however, when she was presiding over her court, not all of us in her large clan were included. She loved some unconditionally, ignored many of us, and treated some as if she despised them. I was always in the middle group, which I think was the best, for, being left alone I learned to observe the goings-on in the family. My Momma was in the ugly stepchildren group with other apparent rejects and Grandma was often vicious toward her. Grandpa Andy went along with all this; Grandma was his boss, too. Momma said that as a child she often watched her beloved poppa hold her sisters in his lap and she would weep as she longed to sit on his lap, to be held and shown love. There was, however, an unspoken but absolute agreement within the family that everyone followed Grandma's lead on everything— including to whom you could show love. So, Momma never felt the love she longed for from her poppa, either. My aunts have expressed utter sadness at being given so much love and special things while Momma was being neglected. They loved their sister, Florence (my mom), who they thought was sweet and smart. But like everyone, they followed Grandma's rules, knowing to cross her meant unbelievable suffering.

Grandma's favorite son was an alcoholic and died of liver disease before he was sixty years old. Grandma, along with the rest of the family, unfairly put the blame for his drinking squarely on his wife's shoulders and defended him. Momma and her sisters talked about how intelligent and wonderful her brother was, no matter how many times he came around drunk. It seemed to me that drinking was a terrible curse in the family and as much as Momma loved her brother, she would not allow him in our house when he was drunk. It nearly broke her heart to turn him away from our door; still, she did several times. It appeared as if Momma felt drunkenness was a contagious disease that would surely taint the family and we'd all come down with it if he came into our home. Alcoholism did run rampant in the Devine clan and it was easy to see that problems often resulted directly or indirectly as a result of it. Yet, this son and Hal were exceptions to the constant belittling of men, which they escaped because they were special to Grandma. Her constant habit, however, of running men down became what I would call a terrible generational curse which most of the women in our family have perfected. Of course, Grandma's strong core belief that "blood is thicker than water" was always in operation too. Those who married into the family were fair game and were often blamed for problems that showed up in our Devine clan. The blame never needed to be based on fact.

No one ever seemed to learn how Grandma's favorites were chosen, but a woman once told me a story of the method used in her family to sort out the special females. When a girl was born, the momma and grandma would inspect her ankles immediately. If the baby's ankles were "thin," she was a favored child; but if the ankles were "thick," the girl was rejected for life. As she told me this story, the two of us, who were obviously fat-ankled babies began laughing and crying uncontrollably at the same time. The complete absurdity of picking the "chosen ones" this way was extremely funny and also very sad. After all, is it even possible to tell thin ankles at birth? I have no doubt that a ridiculous method such as this was operating in our family, under Grandma's direction. You could be attractive, smart and with a great personality, but it made no difference when the standard by which you were judged was something like ankle size or maybe the length of your nose at birth. Whatever standard my grandma had chosen, it was the rule of law and I'm not sure that anyone except Grandma knew what the criteria was. I certainly was not privy to that secret, nor was my Momma. I must admit, though, I was relieved because this story backed up what I had always suspected: Grandma's beloved were not chosen on any type of true merit. Some were good-looking and wonderful, but others were unattractive, rather dumb and without the least bit of charm. It was a mystery, for it was impossible to see one ounce of common sense or logic behind her choices. Despite this, she was able to get everyone to accept her measure on who among us was worthy and who was unworthy.

Grandma was a control freak of the highest order, was always the center of attention and seemed to dominate everything and everyone. An example was Uncle John, who never married and lived with Grandpa and Grandma Devine. He was slow, and she treated him as if he were a poor servant. I wondered if he was mentally challenged or was so beaten down that he acted that way. I asked Momma and my aunts what was wrong with Uncle John, and each gave me the same answer: "Bless his heart, John was dropped on his head when he was a baby and that's why he's so slow." This was the standard answer to why any blood relative was not quite up to par, rather than accept that the family had actually birthed a less than perfect child.

Uncle John was a gentle man and always obeyed Grandma, but I never heard her talk kindly to him, and although everyone else seemed to love him, they rarely talked to him. Uncle John served her loyally and never even seemed to resent it; instead he accepted his lot as the natural order of things. He lived with her until her death, with the exception of a short time when he worked in the WPA (FDR's Works Progress Administration) to build tunnels on the Blue Ridge Parkway. I'm sure she sent him there during the Great Depression to help support the family. No one questioned his situation, but Uncle John was like a captive soul—unable to escape—and my heart always went out to him.

Grandma Devine often decided who her daughters should marry and woe to the one who defied her wishes like Momma did. There are stories of her turning down several of her daughters' suitors because their families were unacceptable to her, despite the fact that our family was on a lower rung of the social ladder in those days. This resulted in at least two extremely unhappy aunts who were obviously married to the wrong men. One of my aunts had married a good man but was still yearning at age eighty for the love of her life—who Grandma had rejected as her husband when she was in her twenties.

One of my uncles disappeared from the family when he was rather young, apparently to get out from under Grandma's control. He hid out thousands of miles away from the family, obviously not wanting to be found. He left a wife and two children and no one knew where he was for many years. Momma often said, "My brother was well-fixed and he made everything good for his family before he left." I learned this meant he had enough money to provide for the family he deserted and had left homes and trust funds in their names. Grandma was mad, but she and the family blamed his wife for his leaving, which was no surprise. I often heard them say, "It was that wife of his. Bless her heart, she's an awful, awful mess, and I don't know why he married her." Afterall, she was not blood.

Thirty years later my cousin located our uncle in Northern California, through his driver's license. He had another family who wasn't aware of his first wife (who he had forgotten to divorce) or of his children by her. When his daughter from the first marriage visited him, he pleaded with her to pretend to be his sister, which she did. Grandma was dead by this time, but many members of the family refused to see him. My Momma loved her brother and visited him soon after he was located. She was at Hal's in California at the time. Momma took the bus because Hal refused to go, stating adamantly, "He left us and hid for years, so if he wants to see me, he'll have to come to me. Otherwise I don't want anything to do with him." Undoubtedly, this man carried a lot of guilt, but he never went back to North Carolina to explain or to apologize. Not too long after this, he died of cancer, and I've always wondered if it wasn't the guilt and the heavy burden of all those secrets that took him. After his death, his wife told his "pretend sister" that she had always known she was his daughter. This secret, along with all the lies, as they usually do, caused a great deal of suffering for many people.

I've always called this uncle "the invisible man" because Momma and others talked about him and how handsome and intelligent he was, but no one in my generation had ever laid eyes on him. He was a vague, shadowy figure who was definitely invisible to us. There were probably many reasons my uncle ran away, and one had to be Grandma's sticking her nose in his life entirely too much. He was more successful financially than most of the family, so she insisted that he help take care of the larger, extended family. This was quite a burden since the country was still struggling with the Great Depression, especially in the South.

*Judy H James*

He had a construction job in Charleston, South Carolina, and the rumor was that he was sleeping with a woman down there. Grandma, who knew everything that happened in the family, got word of the rumor and demanded he stop the affair and come home at once. He returned as ordered but disappeared soon afterwards (minus the lady in question), rather than stay and defy her openly. With Grandma, you went along or you paid the price, as this man did by leaving everything behind and spending a lifetime hiding much of himself from those who loved him. A great deal of the responsibility for the suffering in this family tragedy could be laid at Grandma's feet. The rest falls directly on the head of my dear "invisible" uncle and without a doubt he paid for it at a great cost.

Grandma's rule over the entire family always confounded me no end, as to how she was able to keep such tight control over so many. I don't know why they allowed this, but it says a lot about them as well as her. I know she used all her personal tools of manipulation, including her charm, her smarts, as well as every human weakness that she uncovered in others. She was a bright and determined matriarch and the family accepted this and lived somewhat peacefully, if not happily, under her rule. I've never heard of any face-to-face defiance of Grandma Devine from the "rejects" in the family. Oddly, they actually seemed to worship her and always hoped and prayed to be accepted into her beloved inner circle. However, Grandma never wavered in her choices. Even after her death, her children could not face her faults, and I think it was an indication of the strength of her charisma and fierce determination.

Grandfather Devine was a good man, a faithful and loyal husband, as well as the perfect gentleman. At least that's what I thought most of my life about Grandpa, who rarely talked. In contrast, Grandma Cora talked continuously and was undoubtedly the cock of the walk. I noticed, even when I was quite young, that Grandpa didn't have any say in what occurred and was completely submissive to her. I wondered why he was so quiet; he never even spoke to me.

When I was about sixty-seven years old, I asked my aunt why Grandpa rarely talked. I was totally surprised by her response, for there had not been a hint about the story she revealed, even though my grandparents had been dead for over fifty years.

My aunt reported that when she was a teenager, she saw a boy in church one Sunday who looked very familiar. As soon as she got home she said to Grandma, "Momma, there was a boy in church today who looks just like my brother, Horace."

Grandma shocked her by revealing: "Well, honey, he looks like Horace 'cause he's your half-brother." She said that years earlier, Grandpa had had an affair with her best friend who lived on a farm nearby and the lady had gotten pregnant by him. She was married, and when the boy was born, to everyone's surprise she and her husband raised him. Grandma was furious. I suspect it had less to do with jealousy than with the fact that she had lost control of Grandpa—at least for the time it took for those two to make a baby.

After the affair, grandma let my grandpa know in no uncertain terms that she was the boss, by declaring, "Let me tell you, Levi Andrew Devine, from now on I will rule this roost and you will keep your mouth shut!"

According to my aunt, as a result of his sin he rarely talked and never opposed her. I am positive that Grandma made sure he never forgot his shame for a moment. I asked several cousins if they had heard the story, but this was definitely a well-kept family secret. Evidently, only Momma, my aunts and Grandma's two sexy betrayers knew about it and they had not dared talk for fear of retribution. The sisters had swallowed Grandma's explanation, however, that the affair was the reason for their poppa's silence.

I asked my aunt, who was one of Grandma's favorites (and a lovely, sweet lady who escaped the curse of an unfavored one) if she really believed Grandma was the boss in the family because of the affair.

She laughingly responded, "Well, maybe not. You know Momma was always very strong and Poppa wasn't. He just wanted to get along."

I believe that the affair was how her daughters had justified Grandma's bad behavior all of their lives.

Anyone who knew Grandma Devine had no doubt that she was the captain of that unhappy ship long before Grandpa's indiscretion. Grandma had attended Salem College for a couple of years but had left school to marry Grandpa in spite of her family's objections. At that time, it was unusual for a woman to have attended college, and I think she constantly used her education to dominate. Grandma used his misbehavior to assure her control over a good man with a guilty conscience, and he accepted his punishment quietly. He paid a heavy price for bedding that woman, but he made his own uncomfortable bed and silently slept through life.

I've never known what happened to my half-uncle, and no one in the family seemed to know or show any interest in finding out. I would like to have known how he turned out and if he had a difficult life due to the circumstances of his birth. I wonder too whether or not he knew his real father. I'm sure Grandma ordered everyone to remain silent about him and the entire disgraceful matter. Secrets can be hidden for a time, but they can still have a terrible effect on families and they'll eventually pop up and show their ugly face.

There was another side to Grandma Devine which I never fully appreciated when I was young. She could be quite charming and was a wonderful storyteller. Wherever she was, you could be sure there was high drama—whether it was big stories, good gossip or huge family conflict. She was also well known in the region for telling fortunes and people would come for miles to have her read for them. Grandma drew others to her like a magnet and she always seemed to be surrounded by people. It appeared to me that everyone loved her, except me. If I ever felt any pangs of guilt about not loving her, I would observe her cruelty toward Momma and the guilt melted away like ice in the heat of my anger.

Almost everyone wanted to be included in her inner circle, which did seem magical, looking in from the outside. Even those she rejected were constantly seeking her approval and neither my Momma, maternal aunts or uncles could say anything bad about Grandma. If I mentioned one of her faults, they might agree with me, but would glide over it and quickly relay something fascinating about her. She seemed to be such a powerful life-force that they were completely blinded to her faults - which holds true even now, years after her death in 1950. I still hear others proudly declare, as a badge of honor: "I was Grandma's favorite, and I worshipped her. I didn't even notice her faults because she loved me and thought I was special."

I have observed that those who Grandma Devine loved and spoiled often were weakened by it, those who were disliked often spent a lifetime trying to prove their worth and those of us who were ignored became the observers of life. This was not always true, but in one way or another we were all affected by our place around Grandma's bright light. Many of the beloved felt guilty; the rejected felt lacking and the ignored were frustrated. I don't ever remember her speaking to me or saying a kind word to Momma. There was a great deal of suffering from being trapped in those rigid categories, where we were 'boxed in' and often damaged by the experience.

I still wonder by what method we each got stuck in Grandma's emotionally-charged boxes. My Momma, nevertheless, was a little like her mother, and I confess I was somewhat like Momma, especially when it came to my inability to nurture freely and my control issues. I never knew my Grandma's mother, but I would bet my britches that she had her favorites and was stronger and more controlling than Grandma Devine. I do believe these bad traits have weakened with each generation, and I thank God for that.

As my husband once said, "We're trying to weed out those bad Devine genes in our family line."

I hope we can hold on to the good ones—if we can figure out which are the good genes, and which are the bad ones. It can be tricky.

Now, later in life, I have begun to honor my grandma's good traits, to understand her and to release my bitter resentment toward her. I may never learn to love Grandma Devine, but I have at least begun to see what a complicated and interesting character she was. Grandma was adored by her family, who chose to ignore even her worst faults because she was simply fascinating. She wove her own magic spell and it produced an unbelievably strong web of love, hate and confusion from which we are not yet able to get ourselves completely untangled. She was the true Southern steel magnolia whose influence still touches every member of my family, even those who are unaware of it. Life with Grandma was unpleasant for some of us, but she was quite a character and life around her was never dull. I can't put all blame for the sorrow around us on her because each must take their responsibility; however, there was a lot of pain in our family.

Grandma's influence was not all bad. She was a talented woman, and I know I have some of her good traits too. Life was probably not easy for her as an intelligent, educated woman in a day and time when women were not given much respect by society. I'm also trying to understand that her behavior may have appeared worse from my viewpoint as a small child who felt my Momma was being mistreated. I haven't reached the place where I can see my grandma clearly, but one day I will stop judging her so harshly and be able to truly forgive her and to appreciate her more. Then I will be able to free myself, finally, of all those dark, painful emotions which surround my memories of her.

In the meantime, I try to remember that my Momma truly loved Grandma and never uttered an unkind word about her. I imagine they are together now in that loving, heavenly realm, where I believe Momma receives the motherly love which she yearned for during her earthly life. I also believe she gets to sit on her poppa's lap for a long time while he tells her how much he has always loved her.

# Grandpa and Me

I wish Grandpa
Would talk to me
He only talks to Jack
If he talked
To me
I'd talk back
After all he's
Only a mule named Jack
And I don't think he'll
Ever talk back.

# The Invisible Man

Uncle was a hard-working man
Gave all that he could and
Then he gave her much more than
One good man ever really can.
Everything was a command
From Cora, matriarch of the clan.
The Depression was afoot in the land
But he couldn't any longer stand
Responsibility for all the hungry clan.
So he, without a word to the woman
Or any in the Southern family band
Overnight he became the invisible man.
He left wife and two beautiful children.
It was not at all like this man and
No matter how they searched the land
No one knew until thirty years ran
He crossed the Great Plains and began
Another family near sun and sand.
That's the way he'd defy her demands
This dependable, loving man.
When discovered in sunny, promise land
He could not return to his homeland
For his many hidden secrets he banned
Himself, and soon he was a dead man.

*Judy H James*

Judy and Iris
Hughey
(top)
Becky and
Max Hughey
(bottom)
The only
remaining
childhood photo
of the four
siblings.

Four Siblings: Judy, Max, Becky and Iris.1996

# Moving

# On

# and On

I knew 'up North' was not a good place for Southerners nevertheless, off we went with Daddy to that strange place called New Jersey.

After her injury in the cotton mill, Momma was torn between two bitter enemies who she loved very much. Grandma and Daddy hated each other since both were selfish and always had to be the most important person in the room. As I explained before, when Grandma Devine heard that Momma was going back with Daddy, it would be hard to describe her rage. As Momma told me later, she thought that going with Daddy was the best thing for her family since, "Nothing else looked promising at all." She had five children, no income and no hope for a job because of her injured hand, which would always be slightly deformed. So, she chose to go with Daddy out of pure necessity, and also because she was tired of her children being scattered around in the homes of relatives.

This was about 1942 and our lives changed forever the day Momma decided to go up north with Daddy. Leaving the security of Momma's family was not easy, but she thought this was a new beginning and the dream of reuniting her family. It certainly was a new beginning for us, but not long with Daddy. He'd left us before, after my youngest sister was born. He blamed his leaving on Grandma Devine, who he called a busybody and other names too low-down to repeat. The truth is that Daddy would have left us anyway. He could not cope with staying and supporting a family. We were the second family he had abandoned and there would be another one which he'd make a desperate attempt to leave behind.

Momma had been working in the cotton mill and, as my aunt said, "Bless her heart, Florence sliced her hand wide open on one of those big ol' machines."

I have a picture in my mind of Momma being carried out of the mill on a stretcher, with blood all over her, and I could sense her quiet desperation. We had been living with several of Momma's sisters since Daddy left, and now that she couldn't work we really were at the bottom of the food chain.

It was a time when there were no unions to protect workers in the mill towns. The mills owned everything and everybody, which meant they did exactly as they pleased. It would be years before Momma was paid anything for her injured hand and then it was not much. With a badly damaged hand, for years she had to take work anywhere she could to support us, but for a time she couldn't work at all.

Momma told us, "I'm going to get the law after your daddy and have the judge make him pay all his back child support."

In court, Daddy told a heart wrenching sob story about not having the money and begged the judge to allow him to get his family together and take us home with him. He talked Momma into dropping the case and going to New Jersey where he was living. Of course, this was to get out of paying the child support, for, as we learned, he wasn't interested in keeping his family around. As I said, Grandma Devine was furious and demanded Momma not even consider trusting Daddy. But she felt she had no choice. My aunts said later that they felt powerless to help Momma. This was hard for me to understand and to accept. Momma, on the other hand, seemed to forgive them almost immediately.

All our belongings were tied up in that balled-up sheet, so Momma gathered the four of us (minus Hal), along with our white 'ball of shame' and we crossed the street. She then bathed us in the home of the one brave woman in the neighborhood who was willing to help as we waited for Daddy to pick us up in a taxi. The lady, who was not a relative, also loaned us a suitcase and, thank goodness, we were able to dump that disgraceful, white ball. I'll always remember Momma's humiliation and how utterly alone she was that day as Momma's sisters, many in the extended family and the neighbors just watched. It's hard to understand Grandma's control in those days. Everyone actually feared the possibility of Grandma's terrible rage coming down on their heads if they interfered. I could sense Momma's immense sadness. Despite this, she gave us each a bath before Daddy arrived.

One of her most sacred beliefs, which she often repeated, was: "We may be poor, but we're clean." After all, being poor *and* dirty was her definition of "white trash," so we were always as clean as possible, for fear of sliding even further down the social ladder, into complete disgrace. That lesson to always be as neat and clean as possible stayed with me and is still almost an obsession.

Daddy came, and we were off to the bus station to start a long, miserable trip. It took us much further than we ever wanted to go before it finally ended. We left Momma's family, all the people and places we knew and loved in North Carolina and headed for strange, unknown cities. Although I was very young, I was wise to the fact that nothing ever went well when Daddy was involved. Not only were we trusting Daddy, we were going 'up north' where I had been told nothing good ever happened (at least not for Southerners); nevertheless, off we went with him to that strange place called New Jersey.

The memory of that unhappy bus trip still returns to me when I smell the thick diesel fuel of a bus, and for years it literally made me sick to my stomach.

Our family reunion with Daddy lasted only for a few days; we discovered we were a real problem in his life. We arrived in Patterson, New Jersey, where Daddy left the five of us in a basement room that had standing water on the floor, with one bed in a house belonging to his friend. Then Daddy disappeared.

Upon his return in approximately three days, he dropped a bomb on Momma. He asked her for a divorce. To say the least, Momma was shocked. Daddy, however, had a lady friend, and we were excess baggage that had to go. Obviously, we couldn't return to Momma's family. He was eager to be rid of us, so he quickly put all his excess baggage on a bus, with very little money, and we were off to Virginia. He sent us to live with one of his sisters. It meant another long trip and I thought I was going to die from the sickening odors on that bus. Momma put up a good front on the trip, though we could sense her feelings of desperation. Without a doubt, Daddy and the north had confirmed that my gut was right. I learned never to ignore it and to listen when it spoke to me. The worst part was that Grandma was right - we shouldn't have trusted Daddy.

When we arrived in Virginia needing food and shelter, my irritable and quite odd aunt and her husband were not happy. I don't know if this family had any warning before we were hurled into their lives, but they certainly looked as if they had been ambushed. They already had about five people in their small two-bedroom apartment, and now at least ten of us were living there. Actually, I lost track of the exact number; they had six children, but the older ones would come and go, with at least two visiting occasionally from the Army. At night, the floors were carpeted with bodies and it was noisy like a crowded chicken house. My uncle, who I always thought of as "the hillbilly," was quiet, but obviously resented our presence. I couldn't blame him. I'm surprised he didn't send us packing the next day. Yet, we lived with them for months. As soon as her hand had healed adequately, Momma got a job at the A&P grocery store as a cashier. After some time, she had enough money to rent an adjoining apartment for us.

My aunt was a large, buxom woman who thought more of herself than anyone else. She had many ailments and seemed to want something she could never find. She complained about everything in general and us kids in particular. This lady took care of us when Momma worked, and made it clear she didn't like the job. We tried to stay clear of her. Still, each day when Momma came home, my aunt had a wild tale for her about what we had done - which was usually a surprise to us. Her stories never made much sense, but we were punished to satisfy this troublesome woman because Momma needed her to care for us while she worked. You could say she had us right where she wanted us, including Momma.

Amazingly, her children loved us from the beginning. All of them were kind and thoughtful each time we were thrown back into their home, which was too often during my childhood. They treated us very well, despite their mother, or perhaps because of her. They were a bright spot in our lives and we've always loved them for that.

My aunt dressed in black, from top to bottom, and often wore a big black hat which gave her the appearance of being even larger than she was. She was not a happy person and was hateful toward Iris. This lady was an habitual fainter, was very dramatic and fainted anytime she got frustrated with us or needed attention. She'd do this by putting the back of her hand to her forehead, sighing heavily and, with a couple of pitiful whimpers, she'd slump to the ground. We'd call a neighbor, who'd bring smelling salts that revived her after a time. We didn't believe her faintings were real because they happened too often and at very convenient times. We assumed it was all a part of another drama to attract attention and to blame us.

Once, she fainted outside and was lying flat on her back in the grass, looking like a giant dressed in black. We called someone, threw a glass of water in her face, pretending to revive her, and then stood around giggling. We knew she could hear us, but she was helpless to do anything since, after all, she was unconscious. When revived, she insisted to her pastor who had arrived on the scene that we constantly got on her nerves, and then told him what bad children we were. I don't think he believed her either, since he had been witness to these dramatic scenes before.

I don't think Momma thought the faintings were real either, but nevertheless we got into trouble, which was especially difficult for Iris. She got the worst end of the stick since she was the oldest and had been told to keep us in line. She was punished often and too harshly and, as a result, Iris and our aunt became bitter enemies. My sister often said, "I don't get mad, I get even." She did this in creative ways and often angered the poor woman immensely. My aunt wasn't satisfied with her life before we arrived, and we certainly didn't make her life easier. We did give her ample opportunities to display her seemingly insatiable need for drama and attention, though.

We lived in the apartment next door to them. I'm not sure it should be called an apartment. Woody Park was fashioned from hundreds of old, long and ugly barracks which had been built for servicemen in World War I. After the war, each of the barracks had been made into about four apartments. They had never been painted and looked like long, gray barns without the graceful shape of a barn. These barracks were lined up in a horseshoe shape for many blocks, and together they were known as Woody Park. Many families of soldiers and sailors from bases nearby lived there and most were young people.

It was not a bad neighborhood, though. It was relaxed and fun, with children playing in the dirt yards and Hank Williams' songs and other hillbilly music (which I hated) constantly blaring from open windows in the summer. This was our home, off and on, with Norfolk, Virginia, for seven or eight years in the 1940s.

We actually had some good times in Woody Park. We'd collect bottles, trade pennies and nickels for them and catch a bus to town on Saturday. There was a lot to do and it was cheap. We would watch our heroes, Roy Rogers or Gene Autry, ride, sing and fight. Then we'd argue about which was the best cowboy, the most handsome or had the smartest horse (of course it was Roy Rogers and Trigger). Afterward, we could watch the Three Stooges slap each other around in a movie for five cents at the community center, and then go swimming for free.

I have a great memory of Iris jumping into the community pool and coming out with shiny green hair. She had peroxided her hair the night before and the chlorine in the pool gave her wildly colorful hair, which was unacceptable in those days. I always remember this funny episode when I spot a young person with neon-bright hair these days. You could say Iris was ahead of her time.

When Momma's sister, Aunt Ed, got out of the Women's Army Corps in 1945, she stayed with us for a short time and brought loads of excitement into our home. She had had quite a time during the war, serving in Paris and London, and we loved her wonderful stories. Aunt Ed always brought along the craziest fun, lots of laughter and was a delightful breath of fresh air in our lives which we desperately needed. She was one of Grandma's rejects; despite this, she had a great enthusiasm for life, and we loved her.

This was not an easy period for Momma- with low wages at the A&P, four kids and our relative who delighted in making life difficult for her. My aunt longed to be beautiful and constantly complained that men were flirting with her, which no one ever saw except her and she seemed to be jealous of Momma. Also, she pretended to see no wrong in Daddy and blamed Momma for all of his bad behavior. Sadly, many years later, this lady had mental problems and we should have seen that coming earlier in Virginia. We were kids, however, just trying to enjoy life, which was not always easy. We were striving to make the best of hard times and we did manage to have fun some of the time in spite of everything.

Momma worked long days in the store, six days a week, and didn't make enough money for us to eat very well. Some days we ate peanut butter and crackers for all three meals. At Christmas, the grocery store gave us a large bag of apples and oranges, with nuts on the top, which was our best gift and we loved it. Relatives from North Carolina often sent us hand-me-downs and sparkly, old costume jewelry which we delighted in wearing. Our relatives next door had helped to feed us when we lived with them, but didn't now, especially since their sons had returned from the war and they had an even larger family.

Believe it or not, a few years after the aborted New Jersey reunion, Daddy showed up looking like a dandy-with his empty promises in tow-declaring he was going to stay and get a real home for us. He soon escaped, however, and for many years he continued this habit of coming to our home and making fabulous promises. He'd stay a few days and then skip out in the dark of night, not to be seen again for a year or two. Though he didn't help financially, Momma allowed him to return to our home, off and on, until I was in my teens.

Momma stayed upbeat most of the time and sang songs from the Hit Parade or hymns while doing housework, which she loved. Her favorite song was "Amazing Grace." But I remember the little ditty that made us laugh when she sang it to us:

> Would you like to swing on a star
> Carry moonbeams home in a jar
> Or would you rather be a mule?
> A mule is an animal with large funny ears
> And he'll kick at anything he hears
> He has a stubborn streak, and his brain is weak …
> Or would you rather be a pig?

She always encouraged us to do our best in everything that we did and had us attend the Baptist church every week. Momma taught us that no matter how poor we were, we could become successful with a good education and determination. She didn't become bitter, and never discussed the humiliating time with Grandma or ask why her sisters had deserted her then. She knew Grandma well enough to realize how impossibly difficult life would have been for anyone in her family who might have stepped forward to defend her.

Momma had a saying: "What goes 'round, comes 'round." She knew life would take care of things and there was no need for her to be angry. She forgave all of them much quicker than I thought she should have, which was extremely wise of her.

Eventually, about eight years after leaving North Carolina, when we were desperate we did return to Grandma Devine, who by then was old and sick. Our return occurred because of a short and unfortunate time in Baltimore with a cousin, who had invited Momma there for a business scheme that quickly failed. Sadly, all our meager belongings burned in a suspicious fire in the house in Baltimore while we were on the trip back to North Carolina. Momma never received any insurance money, and we again lived with various relatives. Later we lived with Grandma for a short time but were soon forced to move out of her home because she had cancer. Since Daddy was nowhere to be found and Momma couldn't afford to rent a place, we went to an orphanage called The Home for Motherless Children. It was there, deep in the foothills of the Blue Ridge Mountains that real tragedy came into our lives.

Our leaving the bosom of Momma's family in that small town in North Carolina was probably the best thing that could have happened to us, although it certainly did not seem so at the time. For those years we were no longer under Grandma's thumb, for although we still felt her influence, it was far less. Had we stayed there, we would not have had the many opportunities and experiences that we did from living in larger towns. Virginia was a good place to grow up and provided us a better education than we would have gotten in rural North Carolina. The town we lived in offered a lot of excitement, especially during the war, and we often crossed the Chesapeake Bay by ferry to go to Norfolk to visit Uncle Lawrence and Aunt Lena, with whom we also lived for a short time. Both places were alive with activity, including soldiers and sailors because of several military bases in the surrounding areas. There was also a shipbuilding center in the area, and I remember a ceremony each time a ship was launched. I loved to watch these events; it was incredibly exciting and scary to see those handsome, huge monsters slide into the water with tremendous noise and a mighty splash.

I had rheumatic fever during this time. I had excellent care by the state health department, was diagnosed at Johns Hopkins University and then spent time in the University of Richmond Hospital. I also had the wonderful experience of the foster home where I lived for a year in the beautiful Shenandoah Valley, all courtesy of the state of

Virginia. Leaving North Carolina and the family was a blessing in disguise, even with an unhappy and unpredictable, fainting lady in our lives. At least we were out from under Grandma's constant meddling and her mistreatment, of Momma. Momma never seemed to be mad at Grandma and although she was treated like an evil stepchild, she loved her unconditionally until the day she died.

Events that seem extremely bad at the time can often actually turn out to be for the best, especially if you keep positive. Momma was able to make the best of things, no matter what came our way, and she taught us to never give up. She was not perfect, and, like everyone, she had her faults. Even so, she did a great job raising us. She was able to instill good morals as well as determination and ambition in each of us. Her love and strength through the worst of times far outweighed her shortcomings. Daddy was quite a character, and he made life difficult for those who loved him.

Without a doubt, Momma was an interesting character and fascinating in many ways. It took me years to even become conscious of how her attitude toward me as a child had affected me, but now I know it was exactly what I needed. Momma had lost out on her dreams long ago, so she poured them all into me and my siblings. She was strong and wise in many ways. I am grateful to her for caring so much and I am proud to be her daughter

My Momma's favorite poem of mine:

# Soul's Sunshine

Laughter is the sunshine for the soul
it can make you feel so young
back again in that sweet fold.

Laughter will make an old heart dance
it clears away the cobwebs
and gives life another chance.

Laughter will take away life's ills
so laugh with your loved ones
and get ready to be healed.

In laughter's presence we feel loved
also happy, carefree and
one of the dearly beloved.

# Aunt Ed, the WAC

When I was young she brought joy and love
Sometimes she seemed to come down from above.
We called her Aunt Ed and loved her so
She would bring fun and maybe a hair bow.
She was a doll and was so plucky
But we're the ones who were so lucky
For she laughed, she talked and made much noise
Then she went off to the war with the boys
For even if she'd never come back
She had always wanted to be a WAC
And though in the country she was born
Boy, she looked snappy in that uniform!
She went to Paris and London too
Came to tell of places we never knew
And learned to call the bathroom the loo.
She brought her own sweet music and we knew
That when Ed, the WAC, blew into town
We'd all be happy while she was around.

Dedicated to our lovely WAC,
Aunt Edna Earle Devine Raiola

# Daddy

# Rolling

# Rolling

# On

We're not sure that the three wives and eight children which my daddy claimed to have are really all there are.

*Judy H James*

Daddy was always rolling on, rarely staying in one place, and didn't seem to care enough for anyone to stop for long. He wandered for many years, leaving children, wives and other women strewn in his path. He was a real con man, especially where Momma was concerned. His name was Bryan Odell Hughey, and he claimed he wasn't sure how many times he had been married or how many children he had. He left them behind to wander and sometimes he laughed about this. He was a Scotch/Irish country playboy, and it's possible I have half-siblings spread across the Eastern Seaboard which was his playground. He said he had three wives or maybe more, but we can only prove three wives and eight children, which included Momma and us four children. He abandoned all of them; however, when he attempted to leave his last family he was forced to return.

I think Irish men think of themselves as lovers and rebels and they always seem to be off somewhere fighting, drinking or whatever. Their women complain yet take them back no matter how much pain they bring along and throw into their lap. My Daddy and Momma were like this. Daddy was interesting- he told stories, wrote poems, sang in a quartet, wandered around having one affair after the other, never taking responsibility for anything or anyone. He first left us early in my life. He had already left at least one wife and child before siring us. He returned occasionally, showing up on our doorstep looking dapper in expensive clothes and shiny new shoes. Momma always told me, "Honey, you can tell a lot about a man by his shoes." What those shoes told me was that my daddy was a truly selfish man. Although we were so poor we often didn't have enough food, had to live with relatives and wore hand-me-downs, he showed up, as Momma would say, "Dressed to the nines." Regardless of his promises, which always included our special dream of having our own home, after a few days he'd leave. Daddy would pack up, sneak out in the middle of the night and disappear like a phantom. He rolled in and out of our lives like this for years. He never brought gifts; he only brought a suitcase full of empty promises and heartaches.

Daddy didn't support us, yet every few years I'd look up and there he was again, charming Momma and telling her all the lies she wanted to hear. When he came, he had stories of his adventures and loved having an adoring audience. After many of his "visits," which inevitably meant disappointment, I became angry and refused to believe in him or those elusive dreams. When Daddy was visiting, he'd act as if he were in charge and once slapped my baby sister so hard across the face that her head flew back. I knew he had no right to do that, so I made up my mind that he was not my daddy anymore. After that, I ignored him when he wandered back into our lives from his playground up north. The rest of the family enjoyed his wild tales, and I'd sit outside in the dark until bedtime and then sneak into my bedroom. I wondered why he came to us and I finally decided he needed a rest from his hard living and had nowhere else to go. When rested and bored, he'd wait until we were sleeping and go off to search for greener pastures, or whatever it was he needed so desperately that he had to escape into the dark night.

Momma said she needed help, especially after her hand was injured, and he could always fool her into thinking he would stay and fulfill all her dreams. But I think she liked hearing about his adventures too and it was exciting for her when he was around. She loved him although he abandoned her repeatedly, because Momma really did not believe she was worthy of love. I knew by the time I was seven years old that he would leave again and that she deserved much better than this wayward sometimes-husband.

Of course, Daddy was not in Virginia where we were living, when Momma learned she was pregnant after one of his visits. She decided she couldn't have the baby; it was impossible for her to take time off from work, she'd definitely lose her job and she couldn't possibly afford to feed another child. She knew deep down that Daddy could not be depended on to help, nor could her sisters who were far away and under Grandma's control. My aunt lived next door, but she would have only caused Momma additional problems had she known of the pregnancy. I doubt Momma even knew where to contact Daddy, and there was

*Judy H James*

nobody she could confide in or anyone to comfort her. She did tell my sister Iris, who was a child of about ten years old, which I'm sure was disturbing for her at that age. I didn't know about the abortion then. However, I know this was a horrible decision for Momma to make and she was basically alone. Knowing now how much she loved her children, I'm sure it must have been an unbelievably difficult time for her. This revelation was a shock for me, and my heart ached for Momma when Iris told me, soon after Momma's death. Iris said the doctor who performed the illegal abortion in the mid-1940s also begged Momma to let him adopt Becky, my youngest sister, who was a darling toddler at the time. He was serious, pointing out that he could give her child a much better life than she could provide. Of course, Momma refused, but I suspect, considering her circumstances at the time, that was not an easy decision either.

Momma was a strong, independent woman who fought to provide for her children. But when it came to Daddy, she was weak. Love had always been painful for her and so she desperately held on to the hopeless fantasy of a life with him. Back then, I was completely confused as to why she would let Daddy roam in and out of our lives as he did.

I have come to understand her need to be loved. There was a Cole Porter song that Momma sang a lot in those days:

> You made me love you
> I didn't wanna do it
> I didn't wanna do it.
> You made me happy sometimes
> Sometimes you made me sad
> But there were times dear
> You made me feel so bad!

I didn't know Daddy's mother and father, but I've heard many stories and not an ounce of it was good about either one. Grandma Annie was called "the meanest woman I ever knew" by several people, and Momma led that chorus. I asked her if this grandma was as bad as her mother, Grandma Devine, who was my standard for mean. Momma declared, "Let me tell you, child, your Grandma Hughey took first prize for mean and anyone'll tell you that who was around her for two minutes." This truly was frightening for a girl to have to swallow, knowing that I carried both sets of those mean genes.

Momma said that my two grandmas came once, right after she had a baby, and she almost lost her mind because of their hateful, vicious bickering. One of my regrets in childhood was that I didn't have a sweet, loving grandma who rocked me and sang to me, but it seemed to me that my grandmas only brought dark drama into our lives.

Daddy's father, James Micklebury Hughey, was an itinerant minister and a farmer in South Carolina. Momma said that Daddy told her that each of his sons had threatened to kill him before leaving home as teenagers. I could understand how most of my aunts and uncles came by their weird personality after learning more about their parents. However, one sister, Aunt Carrie, was a sweet and thoughtful lady who was good friends with Momma. One of Daddy's brothers was a kind, sensitive man, but was a lifelong functioning alcoholic. Uncle Lawrence, the brother to whom Daddy was rather close, was a drinker and a loud, brash womanizer like Daddy. It amazed me that one could come from that family as normal and thoughtful as Aunt Carrie, when her siblings were completely messed up.

The Hugheys were smart and interesting, but you had to be wary or you could get caught up in their craziness. For example, at family gatherings, my cousin hypnotized the children to keep them quiet. I never saw this, but others have declared that they witnessed her hypnotize the kids, who slept until it was time to leave. With a snap of her fingers, off they'd go with their parents.

When I was young there was an incident that seemed to hang like a pall over the Hughey clan. This was because of a sad event that occurred when Uncle Marvin's family was visiting his brother, Uncle Lawrence. While they were there, the families went swimming and Uncle Marvin's daughter drowned. I've never known the details or if anyone was blamed for the girl's death. It was rarely talked about openly. This became a secret in the family that everyone knew but talked about only in whispers. That didn't prevent the sadness from affecting the family, though, like things we cannot talk about, often do.

As I've said, Daddy would appear unexpectedly out of nowhere, bringing his huge ego, tall tales and his bag of tricks. Uncle Lawrence would come across the Chesapeake Bay and they'd compete to see who could tell the wildest tales, which became increasingly outrageous as the night proceeded. They tried to outdo each other, especially in their stories about the fights which they'd been in. Each bragged that he had fought the hardest and been the bravest, with both declaring he was the winner in every instance. They often called each other a liar about who was the toughest fighter. It was obviously the greatest badge of honor for these two braggarts, whose main recreations were drinking and fighting. Daddy told one story, declaring, "One man thought he could push me around and I decided to teach him a lesson. I hauled off and socked him so hard that he slid ten feet across a parking lot, right under a car which nearly killed him." Uncle Lawrence swore he had been the one who hit the man- and off they'd go into one of their shouting, cussing, lying and laughing sessions that was their version of fun. It could have actually been an enjoyable show for Momma. Sometimes it lasted long into the night. Ordinarily her life wasn't much fun, so I think she welcomed the amusing drama that these somewhat handsome oddballs brought into her life.

Daddy and his brother both had a chip on their shoulder and each thought he had been wronged by many, especially the "higher-ups." They were usually mad at someone and they'd brag loud and long about how they had outsmarted whomever it was that had tried to get the best of them. This included an abundance of people: doctors, mayors, police officers and bosses, to name only a few. Daddy's favorite story was about a doctor who had told him many times to quit smoking or it would soon kill him. Daddy would laughingly report, "That doctor thought he was so smart and he's already dead. I'm proud to say that I'm still smoking and not about to die." He thought this was hilarious. Like many of his stories, it had a streak of meanness in it. Daddy and his brother loved going up against anyone who had even a hint of authority and telling about these events kept them laughing and obviously quite proud of themselves. I came to believe that perhaps God had invented authority, so my daddy and all Scotch/Irish men could be happy resisting it and bragging about it. I fear that rebelling against authority is in my genes and to this day I can see it showing its ugly, face in my behavior and that of my children.

Daddy had deserted his first wife without ever knowing his son from that marriage. This son, James Hughey, was the long-lost brother that we found late in life, who became a wonderful part of our family. When I was a teenager, Daddy remarried and had three more children and they lived near us after we settled in a small mill town in North Carolina. Even then, he called Momma and talked about his problems, which upset her. We encouraged her to insist that he stop, which was not easy for her. Finally, she was able to do this many years after they were divorced.

Daddy's last wife was a nurse. I'm sure she was the one who supported the family. Although Daddy sold used cars, he spent most of his time sitting around telling jokes, forever trying to impress the locals or anyone who would listen. I had wondered why he had not deserted this family. In time, I learned that he had attempted to escape. His wife's brothers and father, however, went looking for him and forced him at gunpoint to return home. They were a bunch of tough mountaineers and they allegedly told him that if he ever left again they'd hunt him down and kill him. Everyone, especially Daddy, thought they would shoot him, so like it or not, he stayed. I was ashamed, as a teenager, to admit how relieved I was to hear he had tried to leave that family too. Even though I had long given him up as my daddy, if he stayed with them, there was the childish fear that his leaving us may have been our fault. However, by then I was thankful to God that no one had forced him at gunpoint to return permanently to my family.

When young, Daddy was rather good-looking; as he grew older, his face became ugly and pockmarked. I believed in my heart that hard living and a guilty conscience had carved all the ugly marks on Daddy's face and his guilt was popping out for all to see. After his wife died, we visited him more often and although we didn't bring up the past, he was constantly defending himself and denying he had done anything wrong. With great emotion, he once said, "I wanted to take care of you, but your momma turned y'all against me. She lied to you, 'cause I mailed money to her many times for you." We assured him that we would've known about any money that came, since we were home before her each day and opened the mail first.

He also blamed Grandma Devine for keeping him away, saying she hated him. He was right, she hated him, but Grandma had thrown us out of her family when we were young, largely because of him. She wasn't there when Momma had gone with him to New Jersey—only to discover he had a girlfriend and he asked Momma for a divorce. Then he had loaded us, his excess baggage, on the first bus out of town, to a relative's crowded apartment in Virginia.

After Grandma died, when we were in the orphanage, Daddy had promised Momma to get us out of that sad place. Instead, he disappeared. It was difficult to understand how he could defend his actions, but that was another symptom of his inability to accept responsibility or to face facts. Watching him, I learned that a person can lie, convince themselves of anything and eventually they begin to think it is the truth.

Momma was very forgiving, and as we got older she encouraged us to visit Daddy more because she knew that we would have to forgive him, in order to be happy. As he aged, it was unpleasant to be with him, for he seemed to be drowning in the guilt which he could not accept, nor release, and it was painful to watch. Once, Iris told him, "Daddy, if you'll forgive us, we will forgive you." He became angry, his face turned red and he began hollering, "What do you mean? There's nothing for you to forgive me for."

He still told the same stale stories and jokes also, which he laughed at, but there was absolutely no joy in him. Once, when I was with him, he became tearful and asked, "Why don't you love me as much as you do your Momma? I've always loved you, but she's turned y'all against me." It was strange that he could ask me that. But he had his own story, which he desperately held on to. Later he wrote to me, declaring: "I hope the good Lord will strike me dead right now if I was to blame for one thing." That's when I knew God was not a vengeful God, because Daddy lived for at least ten years after that.

Of the three children from Daddy's last marriage, one boy, had mental and physical disabilities. Daddy's only expression of regret came when he told Iris he felt this child was his punishment for the things he had done. But he never really accepted responsibility, and in attempting to blame others he could easily ignore the facts. Later in his life he wrote me a letter in which he said he could not understand why I came to North Carolina to see Momma and did not visit him. He said he thought of committing suicide, which I realized was a plea for pity, and by then he was someone I could no longer hate.

When I was in my sixties, I was asked in a self-development course to write about what my father and mother had each contributed to my life. My first thought was that only Momma had, but I began to realize that Daddy had been a major influence and I decided to search for the positive aspects of his contribution. He was creative in many ways and he sometimes supported the underdog too. I had heard the story of his getting blackballed from the cotton mills in several small Southern towns because he had supported the unions. He and others had tried to organize the mill workers, whose wages were so low they barely eked out a living. Most of them had to plant cotton or take odd jobs to support their families. Supporting the unionization of mill workers was a hopeless mission in the South in those days. But I suspect he was glad he was forced to leave town to get work—he did like to travel. This took courage, though, in a time when the mill owners in the South owned everything and everyone in them, including our ministers.

I realized I did learn a lot from Daddy or because of him. Since he was not there for me as a child, I had to live in many places, including some which were not safe; therefore, I learned to take care of myself. I became independent and resourceful, for which I'm thankful. But the drama and rebellion I saw in Daddy have also been a part of my life. It was also from my Daddy that I learned how to spot a con man from a mile away, which is a handy talent to have. His deceit, however, taught me how lies will always come home to haunt you and also hurt the ones who love you.

Daddy had a certain charm, but he was difficult to love because he betrayed all who cared for him. In the end, he was without love and he was a truly sad person. Even his children who had forgiven him didn't like being with him. He was continually bragging, blaming others and then defending his actions in a one-sided argument that made us uncomfortable. In time, I was able to forgive him and eventually was able to feel real compassion for the man.

At one time, I thought that Daddy only cared for himself, but eventually I discovered the problem was that he didn't love himself. I believe that, like Momma, he felt he was not lovable. He was his own worst enemy, for although many had tried to love him, he wasn't able to give or receive the most important thing in life. He died a miserable man, having missed out on the affection of his many children and wives.

Today, I'm able to see that Daddy's wandering was an attempt to find peace—which I don't think he found. When I was with him, I felt an emptiness within him that he was never able to fill and understanding this helped me to forgive him even more. My sister Iris said to him once, "Daddy, you are the one who really missed out. You not being there just made us closer and made us stronger." Daddy knew this was true, and for a moment I saw a deep sadness move across his face. When I no longer wanted him hurt, he saw his life and what it could have been and he suffered that loss.

Daddy lived until he was almost ninety years old, and I doubt he was truly happy for even one moment. Wherever he is now, I hope he no longer feels that need which drove him to wander relentlessly in a constant search for something he would never find. I do pray he has found peace and has accepted love into his life, for I don't think he did while he was here on earth.

# The Rolling Stone

My daddy was a rolling
rolling stone
And he rolled and rolled
on alone
But for some reason he'd
always, yes
Always come rolling
rolling back
And Momma she never gave him
any flack
When he came rolling, rolling
rolling, back
Then he'd slip out in the middle
of the night
I don't know if it was wrong
or right
But my daddy was truly a
rolling stone
And he never found us to be
his true home
So he kept on moving like a
rolling stone
A man so alone, rolling
rolling, rolling on.

Brothers: Lawrence, Van, Marvin and my father Odell Hughey

Grandmother Cora Akers Devine (top right) with her sister.

(Children unknown)

Paternal grandma,
Annie Goforth Hughey

My father, Bryan Odell Hughey

My father with his first
wife Kate Ford and my
half brother Jimmy
1934

The Hughey Family. My father Odell is second from the left. 1934

# My Lovely

# (Lonely)

# Foster

# Home

Christmas was the loneliest time of this year, for I longed to be at home with my brothers and sisters by our little Christmas tree.

I lived in a foster home without seeing Momma or any of my family for a year in 1945, when I was seven years old. I learned what Dickens meant when he wrote: "It was the best of times, it was the worst of times." My time in a foster home as a child could have been very sad, but it actually turned out to be one of the most wonderful times in my childhood. At the same time, it was sometimes lonely too. I had been diagnosed with rheumatic fever and there was no one to care for me at home. Momma had to work, and Iris, who had stayed home with me for a while, was required to go to school, of course. So, the Virginia Health Department decided I should be placed in a foster home in order to get the care that I needed. Momma reluctantly agreed because she knew it was best for me. Of course, Daddy wasn't around to help her with this decision, either.

Momma and I rode a Greyhound bus from the coast, west to the mountains. This trip was not one I thought would be happy, but as we glided through that wonderful scenery, I developed an abiding love for those magical mountains. Spring was in the process of clothing the never-ending blue waves of mountains in fabulous colors. Black, brown and white cows and horses were roaming green hills spread with yellow dandelions. All of this loveliness was framed by handsome, rugged, cross-rail fences. Adding to the wonder of it all, the rocky Natural Bridge appeared high up across the road in front of us, and I shivered with delight when we rode under it.

For me it was all like heaven. I loved having my Momma all to myself, which was rare although I knew she'd soon have to leave me for a very long time. We got off the bus in Staunton, Virginia, and spent the night in a dumpy little motel. I can still see the motel light flashing on and off outside the window, first lighting up and then darkening my Momma's sad face. I was nervous, even though I was used to being left in strange places. I had lived with many relatives and had recently spent about three months alone in the hospital in Richmond. I knew Momma couldn't afford to visit me during the year I was to be there, but despite this, it was difficult knowing it would be a very long time before I saw her again.

The next day we continued on to a lovely little community nearby which was to be my home for the next twelve months. I recall crossing a small wooden bridge with water splashing over the rocks below, and smooth, green pastures rising up fast on each side of the creek. It seemed to me that we slid deeper and deeper into beauty as those awesome mountains surrounded us. After we crossed the rustic bridge, the little hamlet of Bridgewater came into view and I knew immediately it was the most peaceful and wonderful place in which I would ever live. The hamlet was in the Shenandoah Valley of Virginia, the most beautiful part of the awesome Blue Ridge Mountains.

Momma had to leave quickly and return home. I don't recall her leaving, though; I think it was too painful for me. I do remember that when I arrived at the home, another girl my age was living there who was also a foster child. I was thankful that she left soon; she was extremely jealous of me and I didn't want her there either. I was going to take her place, which was difficult for her, and later I could understand because I would never have wanted to share my special time there with another child.

The two women who took care of me were old maids- each about forty-five years old, give or take a few. They were sisters, and I don't think I ever knew their full names. The home was a large, two-story brick house sitting on a high knoll and surrounded by hills, pastures and rushing mountain creeks. There were many outbuildings for chickens and rabbits, and others for storing meats and canned goods. It was an exciting place for me and I loved this heavenly mountain retreat. I had never known such abundance and peacefulness, therefore I quickly settled into my new home. My room was an old, delightful, glass greenhouse from which I could see the apple blossoms in the spring, white-topped mountains in the summer, as well as the vivid colors of a mountain autumn. In the winter the snowflakes surrounded me on the glass and at times I could lie in bed and study the stars or almost feel the rain but never get wet.

It was warm, cozy and private—but at first it was a bit lonely. It took some time for me to get used to sleeping in a room alone, without having to fight for the covers with my sisters, brother or cousins. Before long, I loved everything about this place.

My foster mothers, who I'll name Miss Sweet Farm Lady and Miss Tall Dark Teacher, were both fascinating women in their own right. However, they were so different it was hard to imagine they were sisters. To my surprise, for some reason they absolutely refused to speak to each other. They communicated only by writing notes and I was sometimes pulled into service to deliver their messages. Their father had left them this large family estate, which was an active farm, and they supplemented their income by taking in children. There was a great deal of work on the farm since they had to care for apple orchards, chickens, rabbits, cows and me. One sister, however, did all the farm work and cared for me, and the other was a schoolteacher in the local elementary school. They appeared to have some sort of silent agreement as to each sister's job description and, as far as I could see, they never dared cross over into each other's sacred territory.

Miss Teacher was tall, thin and constantly looked like she had eaten one of the sour apples out back of the house. She wore only black dresses and a large hat of the same color. I don't know if she wore it in the classroom, but she always had it on when she came home. I imagined her in class with that big black hat on, in front of thirty scared kids. Life was more formal then and she was more formal than most people, especially there in the mountains. She came into the house each evening and went straight up the stairs to her floor, without a word to anyone. As she ascended those stairs, her head held high, topped off by the hat and all that black, she looked extremely tall and elegant … but a little like a witch, too.

She took her meals in her rooms, which I sometimes carried up to her. Miss Farm Lady and I ate in the huge farmhouse kitchen. I never learned to truly like her, but I was not afraid of the upstairs sister, either. Actually, I had a certain amount of respect for the stately, witchy lady in black.

I think she considered me part enemy since I spent most of my time with Miss Farm Lady. I don't remember her speaking to me, yet she never acted as if she didn't like me—although she ignored me as best she could. She only watched over me at a distance when farm sister went into town for supplies. By no stretch of the imagination did that include being nice to me. It was a necessary duty that she performed without speaking, and I didn't take it personally since I accepted that the sisters' silent agreement somehow extended to me. I had thought that Miss Tall Dark Teacher would tutor me, but she didn't, and I never thought I could ask for it.

No one tutored me during that year, or the next, so I missed the second and third grades.

When I returned to school, the authorities wanted to place me in the second grade. I was very mature and well-developed for my age at nine and knew I would be humiliated with seven-year-old children. I begged them to put me into the fourth grade and promised to do my very best. After much discussion they reluctantly agreed and warned that I would be returned to the lower grade if I did not work up to par. I made good grades because I loved school and due to that awful threat hanging over my head. I knew I could be demoted and placed back with short, little kids, where I would look like a female giant. Thankfully, I never heard about a demotion again. But I knew they were watching me that year.

Miss Sweet Farm Lady, of course, was my favorite foster mother and was the opposite of Miss Tall Dark Teacher. She looked like a farmer and was not at all attractive; she was short, stout, broad-shouldered and strong as a bull. I don't think she had ever worn makeup or cared for her hair, which was gray, straight and wiry-looking. She was, however, the most kind and loving person I had ever known. She was a nurturing, substitute mother and acted as if I were the most wonderful child who had been dropped down from heaven and delivered to her. She made me feel that I was special and the smartest, most delightful person she had ever known. I had a great need for this since, although most of the time I thought that Momma loved me, she could never genuinely show her love to me. When I was a teenager, I asked her why she didn't hold me the way she did my baby sister, and her response was, "You have always seemed so independent that I didn't think you needed it." During this year, Miss Sweet Farm Lady made up for the nurturing that I had wanted so much from Momma.

I went everywhere that I could with my farm lady when she performed her chores. We cut dandelion greens in the pasture, churned butter, made cheese and fed the many animals, and I helped as much as I could. I didn't ever try to take advantage of Miss Farm Lady, for I realized that she was gentle but also tough as nails. She was one person in my life that I never challenged, and I felt no need to do so. I was free from school and lived in paradise and I enjoyed it tremendously. She fed me fresh food and milk which was delivered daily from the farms surrounding us. She also saw to it that I drank the medicinal-tasting Ovaltine, which was a drink supposedly socked full of vitamins. The doctor said I must have it daily, and I drank it obediently even though it tasted awful. At home, we often did not have enough food and since rheumatic fever was believed to be caused by a lack of adequate nutrition, she pumped me full of healthy food, which I didn't realize then was organic to the last drop. I went home chubby, healthy and self-confident, and I've never recovered from any of these conditions.

Chicken houses sat out on the back forty, and I often helped feed the chickens and bring in the eggs. To this day, seventy years plus later, pleasant memories sweep over me when I smell wet straw, which was always on the floor of the chicken houses. As you can imagine, the smell of wet straw in a chicken house is not pleasant; nevertheless, my memories connected to this smell have always been. I can still see Miss Farm Lady in her old down-stuffed jacket, long denim skirt and farm boots, teaching me how to care for chickens. So far, I have not found my chicken skills useful in life. Still, every moment I spent with her was valuable to me.

I have wonderful memories of my time there. I played in the creek, ran from the bull, picked an apple and ate it as I played alongside the birds inside the thick hedges that ran down each side of the long brick walkway in front of the house. Everything was fun, even though I played alone, because I was in a happy place. I felt safe and without any worries for the first time that I could ever remember. On rare occasions, we crossed the road and climbed up to the sheep farm on the mountain nearby. I played with the children and watched the farmer shear the sheep, which bleated as if he were killing them. On one visit, the children decided to get boards and slide down the huge hill in front of the barn. We had a delightful time laughing and sliding - until Miss Farm Lady came running out of the house, shouting that I was sick and wasn't allowed to play like that. She grabbed me up, took me home and made me rest and read in my sunny greenhouse. Miss Farm Lady took her responsibility for my care very seriously. That was one time I thought she could have let up a little bit on the caretaking and let me enjoy being with other children. She never did ease off, though, for I had been placed in her care and she saw to it that I got well.

Christmas was the loneliest time of my year, for I longed to be at home with my brother and sisters, around our little Christmas tree. We rarely had more than nuts and fruit from the grocery store where Momma worked, yet she had that day off, and I knew they were all together at home and I wanted to be there. I had received a big box from home. It only made me sad as I gazed at it, sitting beside my bed, waiting for Christmas Day. I don't remember anything that was in that box, but I do recall it made me feel utterly alone because it was from home -where I could not go. At times like this, I wondered if I could ever really go home again.

My favorite memories of the foster home took place in the big kitchen of the farmhouse. I sat on the window seat, drinking hot Ovaltine and talking with my foster mother as she churned butter or washed the dandelion greens, we had harvested from the cow pasture. If I had spent more than a year with her, I probably would have been spoiled rotten. Somehow, the time there merely filled me with a love for life. Momma always expected me to do extremely well, which gave me the ambition I needed to achieve my goals in life. So, I got the best from my two mothers. I have always been very grateful to Miss Farm Lady for that unbelievably lovely year with her. It was early 1945 and it was a peaceful time back in those mountains, despite the war raging in lands far away.

I went back to that house many years later, hoping to see the sisters, but they had passed away by then and the house was in terrible condition. I felt guilty for not having returned sooner to thank them both for sharing their home with me and restoring my health. I learned that sometime after I left, they had opened a day-school together that served proper young ladies. Perhaps they started the school after Miss Farm Lady could no longer continue the hard work of maintaining a farm or Miss Tall Teacher had retired from the classroom. I did wonder if they were on speaking terms during this school venture. I suspect they divided the responsibilities along strict lines, wrote longer notes and had many proper young ladies to deliver them.

Miss Sweet Farm Lady and the foster home served as my serene nest in the arms of the mountains that I came to love and have used as a retreat throughout my life. I benefitted from the many months of nurturing and great nutrition, with a foster mother I adored. Even today, seventy years or more later, the smell of straw, seeing the mountains, or spotting a beautiful brick home returns me there with a flood of lovely emotions. It was a place where I felt truly secure and loved unconditionally. This was often lacking in my childhood, especially in the orphanage, so I carried these memories with me, calling on them when I needed to feel safe and happy. Many memories have faded over the years, yet the feelings have never left my heart. I know I was fortunate to have had a magical time like this, and I sincerely wish it for every child who has a need for nurturing and a little magic in their life.

Momma came for me in a year, and I was able to take a pet rabbit with me, which died soon after my return home. In a way, its death seemed symbolic of the end of an era in my life. As I returned to the family, I was fearful they would not accept me back as a natural part of the family. I had been gone a great deal and my experiences were so different that, truthfully, I never completely felt a part of my family. They thought I was arrogant, and I felt they looked on me as an outsider. Sometimes they treated me as 'special' and other times they resented me, but I was always the outsider and I was confused by this. Whatever the reason for my feelings of being different, I do accept it was partially my fault. To this day, my siblings and I have conflicting ideas on almost everything. Over the years we've been learning to accept each other because of Momma's love for us and our strong family ties.

It is impossible to express how grateful I am to the sisters and to those lovely mountains that brought serenity, beauty and peace into my life. I appreciate having had that amazing year, for I needed the stability and the many wonders that it brought me as a child. Thinking back on this time and experience, I realize I wanted it so much that it was my own dream come true. I believe our dreams do come true when we truly believe in them. And how wonderful that is to know.

# Mountain Resonance

The heartbeat of the mountains joins the beat of my heart
In unison, like the creation from whence
I came.
All the sounds of the giant peaks pulse through my body
I'm revived by nature here in the peaks and valleys
As trees gather diamond raindrops to dance on their leaves
And leaf patterns like green lace are
framed against white clouds
Mystery sounds from waterfalls glide through the moist air
Water flows over the slick rocks to
smooth them for my ride
As ancient forests whisper stories of the past
to me.
I find my soul responding to the Blue Ridge Mountains
The sweet angels of my life reside here in
the mist
Sending love at each twilight to rest within
my heart
I hear music in the sunrise and in the
setting sun
Birds play their sweet songs way into
the night
As the blue, smoky mist fits itself around
(continued)

the ridges.
The energy of these ancient mountains is a part of my being
The rivers and waterfalls, all nature, speak
to me
The serenity of these ageless hills inspires me
each day and
In the many layers of dark, blue waves of
mountain ranges
With all of God's beauty shining
from their wondrous peaks
I lose myself and find my heart, my soul
my purpose.

# Big Box from Home

So far away I'd been forced to roam
I remember that big box from home.
Many months, it seemed so very many
I had been without my family—not any.

Like other children I wanted to be
With family by our Christmas tree.
The lady was really kind and dear
Nursed and nurtured me for a year.

She gave me so much loving care
But still in the heart deeply there
A need to return to my family home
And that box made me feel so alone.

Christmas was just a week or so away
Could I await the wondrous day?
The box had arrived there just for me
From a family I could not see.

Another six months was oh, so long
And when I go back would I belong?
I was seven when I had to go away
Couldn't return for a year and a day.

Stayed in a hospital and the foster home
Went back home and continued to roam.
Positive things came from all the change
I became adaptable in every range.

That big box came to me from home
And I knew I would return not alone
Because my family despite many a tear
Held each member always dear.

That's what my momma's love did do
A big box from home can remind you too
Of that lasting and purest love
Which came through her and from above.

# Sweet Sisters

There once were two sisters, who
Lived on the family estate and grew
Chickens, cows and children too
They were old maids but oh, so sweet
Really, the two were both a treat
But to each other they could not speak.

Their father left Sisters all they had
Except for children and they were sad.
So they borrowed many a lass and lad
From other people who were really down
Yes, the two dear Sisters they found
The children and brought them around.

Two Sisters cared for the children so well
The chickens, cows and estate as well
But their darn feud they would not quell.
They cared for children many years
Saw them through their many tears
Watched them leave despite their fears.

Sisters gave so much to this world
A banner for them should be furled
But these two very Southern girls
Went to the grave not making peace.

*White Trash Warm Hearts*

Maybe up there on heavenly peaks
Sisters will decide who first speaks.

Then God and all will be so glad
For Sweet Sisters were not at all bad
If anything, they were just a little sad
Cause father he had just wanted a boy
Who he'd name after Uncle Roy
Then give him the farm and all its toys.

I was cared for by the sisters
deep in Virginia's Blue Ridge Mountains, in
lovely, bucolic Bridgewater, Virginia.
1945

# Murder at

# The Home for
# Motherless Children

He lay there big, cold and dead, looking as innocent as a preacher on Sunday morning, but I didn't think he was so innocent.

Two terrible murders occurred while I was living in that sad orphanage called "The Home for Motherless Children." The home was in a remote community in the foothills of the Appalachian Mountains and it was there that two boys, Hugh and Billy Ray, shot and killed the head of the orphanage, Professor Sweat. Still not finished, they went looking for Wade, a younger boy, and killed him too. These murders were frightening for the entire community and especially for us children. We lost three familiar classmates as well as an important and ever-present adult in our lives in one awful night. We had, however, lost so much more for those two shots completely shattered any feeling of safety we may have had. Then true fear moved into our lives.

The first time I learned I was going there, my sixth-grade teacher stood up in class and, to my surprise, announced: "Judy's leaving us today. She's going to Union Mills to live in the orphanage." I could not believe what she had just said since no one had even mentioned this to me before. Momma had not told me that we were moving again, and I'd heard nothing about an orphanage. This was to be the sixth school I would attend in that year and I hated to be moving again. Later when I asked Momma why she hadn't told me, she said she was so upset about having to take us there that she simply couldn't bear to tell us.

In a state of shock, I felt pain welling up in my chest as I walked to the front of the room. I was humiliated and wanted to cry, but I refused to let myself. I could feel the stares of the other kids burning into my back as I stepped out into the cold world. Outside, I got into a minister's car with Momma, my brother and two sisters. The plan was for him to drive us directly to the orphanage - no goodbyes, no fare-you-wells from friends or family. This was one more of our many moves. I had thought we were settled in Shelby, North Carolina, with Momma's extended family after Grandma had allowed us to return. I wondered then if I would ever know a stable home where I could make friends and feel a part of a real family. I'd have a long wait for this dream to catch up with me.

A few of the many other places I had been forced to live in my life were sad, but the orphanage definitely was the worst - even before the murders occurred. It was a home for orphans, and I knew I did not belong there. I was not an orphan, although I must admit I was homeless. Momma placed us there because we had nowhere else to go when we were forced to leave Grandma's house because she was dying of cancer. We didn't know where Daddy was, but as usual he was gallivanting around fancy-free, somewhere on the Eastern Seaboard, and failed to show up for us, again.

A minister at one of the many Baptist churches in Shelby, who I had never seen before, drove us to the orphanage. His car felt like a cage to me as we rode silently through winter-brown hills and I blamed him for our having to go to the orphanage. I confess I disliked Baptist ministers intensely from that moment on. After all, he had arranged for us to go to that awful place and had driven us there in his big, shiny, locked car from which there was no escape. He may not have known that the orphanage was a cold and loveless place, but I felt he should have known. It was filled with hundreds of children who yearned for love and nurturing but few found it. So many of the house mothers were bitter, unhappy women who were anything but attractive and could not have gotten hired anywhere else. Many children ran away, searching for their mommas, like my sister Becky did, crying, "Momma, Momma, please come get me." But she couldn't come, and the children were always tracked down by some of the boys or male staff members and the dogs, and then brought back to that sad place. She ran away more than once and I remember feeling so sad for my baby sister who was only eight (8) years old.

I felt it was a very dreary place even before the killings. My two sisters, my brother and I were living in separate "cottages" in the orphanage when the tragedy brought more misery. We had been in the orphanage since 1949, and it was in 1951 that these terrible events occurred. Everyone said they were the most horrible murders they had ever known.

It was on a raw, windy night in March when two friends, Hugh and Billy Ray, borrowed a .22 rifle from their coach, telling him, "We're going to shoot some rats." They went to the school and waited in a dark stairwell for Professor Sweat. When he came out of his office, Hugh ran toward him, pointed the rifle and shot him directly in the face. Another teenager later said that he saw Professor Sweat come stumbling out of the building, blood gushing from his face and running down over his large frame. He was crying over and over, "Oh my God, oh my God, help me, help me." The student said that he was so terrified he ran to his dorm room and hid under his bed all night. They found Professor Sweat lying in the yard, still alive, suffering and bleeding heavily. He died in the hospital hours later, around midnight.

After this shooting, Hugh and BillyRay ran from the building and went looking for fifteen-year-old Wade who was Billy Ray's roommate. Billy was mad because he thought Wade had reported them for smoking and being out at night, which caused them to be punished by Sweat. Pulling Wade from his room, they dragged him to "smoky hollow", a shadowy spot in the woods where students would hide to smoke. Wade swore he hadn't told on them, but Billy Ray didn't believe him and grabbed the gun and, in a rage, shot Wade in the chest. Mercifully, he died instantly from that hateful shot directly to the heart. I don't remember a funeral for Wade and I'm not sure there was one.

According to a campus rumor, Wade shouldn't have been in the home. Allegedly, he had been brought there as an infant, even though the policy was to take in only children who were at least two years old. His mother, father and brother supposedly lived nearby, but it was a big mystery as to why he was not living with his family. I've never learned the truth to Wade's story, but it became obvious to me that bad things do happen to the innocent and it's not always clear why.

All of us living in the home were extremely confused about the murders. The "killers" lived among us and we thought we knew them, especially Hugh, who was mild-mannered and polite. Professor Sweat, highly respected in the community, had been the head of the orphanage for twenty-five years. Although it was sponsored and partly financed by a group of local churches, Sweat was in charge, and he definitely ruled over that campus and everyone there. Some of the kids loved him and some did not. I believed it depended on how bad your life had been before you came to the orphanage. Many of the children had come from terrible situations of abuse, neglect and possibly hunger. Professor Sweat had taken them in, fed them and given them a place to live, so any toughness was softened by how badly life had knocked them around before. He had saved their lives and they thought of him as their savior. I felt however that Sweat enjoyed his power over all the campus too much. He was the one who disciplined and punished everyone, and because he was large, with a big, booming voice, many were afraid of him. He had total control over his little kingdom and he let us know this as he barked out his orders. Big, tall and large-chested, the man always reminded me of a bull elephant as he stomped around maintaining order over his territory.

The rumor was that Professor Sweat had whipped Hugh's girlfriend one night and that Hugh was furious about this. Also prior to the murders, he had told a friend that he wanted to marry his girlfriend when he graduated in a few months; however, since she was younger, she needed permission. He said that Hugh had told him that when he asked Professor Sweat, he became extremely angry and had supposedly yelled, "I will not ever allow you to marry her because she is a prostitute." According to the rumor, he told Hugh that prior to coming to the orphanage she had been a prostitute on the streets of Atlanta declaring, "She will ruin your life." They said that according to Hugh, Sweat absolutely refused to give his permission for them to marry. Hugh became enraged and went looking for Billy Ray, who was also furious because he'd been punished for violating curfew. Together they decided to borrow a gun and get revenge. When he was arrested, Hugh only told the police that Professor Sweat had jumped on him about his girlfriend, which had made him angry, and he didn't give any details. Much of the rumors were never spoken outside the campus, but the students had heard them soon after the murders. Some students did not believe the rumors, but many did. People in the community probably would not have believed them since they respected Sweat. There was an awful mood in the county and much of North Carolina toward these boys, who were immediately labeled as "monsters".

All of us had known Wade, the young victim, as a thoughtful, sweet boy. It turned out that he had not told on them. A teacher testified at the trial that she had seen them after curfew with their girlfriends and had reported both Hugh and Billy Ray. Wade became less than a footnote in the story, though, while everyone praised Professor Sweat and turned their hatred toward the two boys who had killed him. They hardly mentioned the innocent young victim whose entire short life had been spent in the orphanage, although it appeared that he could have been at home with his mother. Many guessed as to why he was not allowed to live with the family, but no one knew the facts.

The murderers were boys who we had seen in the dining room every day and who had grown up alongside us. Hugh was quiet and the most popular boy on campus, as president of the student body and an honor student, but he did seem to have a blanket of sadness covering him. My sister, Iris said he had a job taking care of the furnace near the "baby cottage," where she cared for children. The furnace was in a basement, and she reported that he went there each evening and she heard him singing the same song as he worked:

> "Mona Lisa, Mona Lisa
> Men have named you
> You're so like the lady with the mystic smile.
> Is it only cause you're lonely
> They have blamed you
> For that Mona Lisa strangeness in your smile?
> Do you smile to tempt a lover, Mona Lisa
> Or is this your way to hide a broken heart?

Max, my brother said he heard him sing this song many times as well. Hugh became his idol because he allowed the younger boys to take apples from the cellar where he also worked. Hugh had a lot of potential, but he'd had a very unhappy, unstable life before coming to the orphanage. After his parents' deaths, when he was quite young, he had been shifted around to numerous relatives and foster homes where he felt unwanted. His brother, who lived in California, reported that he had heavy bouts of deep depression as a child and had tried to commit suicide several times because he felt unloved and was very lonely.

Billy Ray's personality was the opposite of Hugh's and his life had been even more tragic. When very young, he had watched as his father killed his mother and then shot himself. He, too, had been passed around most of his life, feeling unwanted and resented by those with whom he was forced to live. Billy Ray might have been handsome if not for the anger that marked his face. He had become a teenager full of rage and we had seen that rage spill over, often on campus. He had numerous angry fights, causing all of us to be wary of him. These two boys were exploding time bombs that awful night in 1951, and afterwards, life was shattered for them and many others too.

I knew there was no sensible explanation for what Hugh and Billy Ray had done, but I could understand how their anger and pain, seething within for years, had burst forth into teenage madness. When their defense attorneys asked to have the two boys examined by a psychiatrist, the judge denied it. This was difficult to understand, but the community had already judged them as evil and wanted to see these two boys punished without delay. The judge who presided over their trials gave them the maximum sentence of life in prison without parole. As he sentenced them, he declared dramatically, "This shocks the moral senses of all people who believe in law, order and constitutional authority." Both boys were under eighteen—Billy Ray was barely sixteen. It was surprising they were not sentenced to death despite the law, because of the mood in the community. Tragically, Hugh was sentenced on the day, at almost the same time that he would have received his high school diploma, with honors, from his victim, Professor Sweat. The headlines in several newspapers read, "Orphan Sentenced to Life for Killing the Director of Orphanage."

Professor Sweat was praised and made into a martyr after his death. On the other hand, Hugh and Billy Ray were called "evil monsters" by everybody, and Wade was ignored. We knew the two boys deserved punishment, but for many of us in the home, the facts were blurred by a rush of childish emotions and frightening feelings. Nothing was completely clear to us in all the confusion.

Momma came to see us, and we begged her to go to the county jail and visit the boys. Billy Ray refused to see her. She took them both white shirts for their trials.

Hugh pleaded with her to take a message to us: "Tell them to remember me and that I'm not a monster." While in jail, he tried to commit suicide by slitting his wrists.

The students had vastly different reactions to Professor Sweat's death. Some mourned him, having seen him as a father figure who had taken them in when they were lost and alone. Sadly, others felt he deserved his fate. That was what I thought, despite many people and the newspapers telling us what a great man he was. My brother, Max was ten and lived in the younger boys' dorm on campus. He recalls that when the house matron told them that Professor Sweat was dead, the group of boys broke out in loud cheers. I have no doubt that similar things happened in other dorms on the campus, but there were also many children who wept for him. All of us, however, were confused and scared because four people who had been a part of our lives were now either dead or in jail.

The day of Professor Sweat's funeral was a rainy March day. Our housemother, an unhappy person, was now even more miserable as she announced that we were going to his wake one evening. She walked all the girls in our dorm through the mud, to the big, white plantation style house that had been off-limits to students before this. It was where he and his wife had lived and where he now lay in his coffin. A heavy depression hung over us as we walked through the dark night to see that dead man. I didn't want to see him, dead or alive, but I had no choice, so I marched by the coffin with the others. He still looked huge to me, wearing the same blue suit, tie and white shirt which had announced to all, "I'm in charge, and don't forget it."

The dark scar under his left eye where the shot had torn into his face was almost hidden, but I could see it. It was eerie seeing him that way, so silent, in such contrast to that loud, larger-than-life man we had seen constantly strutting around campus. He lay there, big, cold and dead, looking as innocent as a preacher on Sunday morning. I thought he was where he deserved to be—in that coffin. But I was a confused and scared twelve-year-old child with many wild emotions roiling around inside me

(I must confess I'm not positive if going to that awful wake and seeing Professor Sweat dead in his coffin was an actual experience or not. It may have been one of my many nightmares; yet, it is still a vivid memory.)

For many years I was in secret turmoil and sometimes felt guilty for thinking Professor Sweat's death was his own fault. The town had made Sweat into a saint, while making our classmates out to be completely evil. I knew no one in this awful event was all evil and no one was without fault. The exception, however, was Wade, an innocent kid who had gotten caught up in this explosion of anger. Everyone said the professor was wonderful and that he had sacrificed for children all his life. Many of us who knew him as a disciplinarian and were often fearful of him, felt that he shouldn't be made to look as if he were perfect or a saint.

*Judy H James*

The media, the orphanage staff and the local churches told only one side of the story, although there was another side which no one seemed to consider. I wanted to scream that there were no saints or monsters in this awful tragedy, but I could not possibly have expressed that at the time. I knew it would have upset many people, especially those who were in control of my life. They would have punished me while making me into a terrible traitor in that small world I had to live in. So, like many of the other children, I kept quiet, with my emotions wound up like a tight ball inside. This was another tragedy: it caused many of us to close down and hide our emotions for a long time.

We had lost four people through violence, and Professor Sweat had even fallen within yards of my dorm window, so we were frightened. We were overwhelmed too, but no one talked about it with us. I realize that the adults were in shock too, but if a counselor had been brought to the school for us, it would have been helpful. My siblings and I did get to talk with Momma when she could come, but it was not often enough. If we could have talked to someone objective on a regular basis, it could have calmed our fears. No one even tried to explain to us how this terrible thing could have happened. Instead, we had to push it down inside, where it would hide for years and, like a worm, eat away at our happiness.

As adults, some of us did face this awful event from our childhood, while others could not even speak of it. Approximately fifty years after the murders, I finally decided it was necessary for me to face these four, lingering ghosts of my past. As a child, I had sworn that I would never go back to that orphanage. Now I knew I would have to go there to confront the fear, guilt and other emotions in order to deal with them where they first surfaced.

I couldn't talk any of my siblings into going with me, so I drove alone. The first time I went, it took tremendous determination for me to drive back into that remote mountain community. There was a heaviness in my chest and it felt like I was descending into darkness. The orphanage had been closed for years. I found Professor Sweat's large, handsome gravestone in the Baptist church cemetery. Then I discovered Wade's small marker nearby, and the sadness I felt overwhelmed me. This innocent boy who had been abandoned as an infant had not even been allowed to grow to manhood. I wondered what his family thought about his murder, since, if he had been with them, it would never have happened. If his mother lived nearby, she must have been heartbroken and ravaged with guilt.

As I stood facing Professor Sweat's grave with Wade close by, I broke down and cried uncontrollably. I couldn't understand why. Then I realized I was releasing a huge burden that I had carried for too long. First, there was my resentment toward a Christian community for the unjust labeling of Hugh and Billy Ray as evil monsters. They had never provided them assistance for their many emotional problems, nor was there professional help for us following the tragedy. Even heavier was my own guilt that had grown and festered over the years, from my blaming Professor Sweat for his own murder. I thought I hated that man, but as a child I saw everything as black-and-white and he had seemed a disturbing presence. Standing at that grave with his image vivid in my mind, I knew no one deserved to die the way he did, especially at the hands of boys who had been cared for and fed at his table. With this awareness, I was able to face and come to terms with my feelings of guilt around the murders. They had been hidden so deep within that I had barely been aware I was holding them inside and that they had affected my entire life. By releasing the pain and crying freely, I began to let go of that heavy emotional burden and I found tremendous relief. My healing and a time of forgiveness began for me. Afterwards, looking around the wooded campus, I suddenly saw the beauty of the green forests and the soft, rolling hills that once had seemed like a bleak, scary place to me. I realized too that it is truly amazing what our minds can do to us especially as children when alone.

As I drove around the nearby community, I tried to talk with those who were residents in the home with me. I found that even a half-century later, many of these adults found it too disturbing to talk about the murders. One woman hid in her house, peeping out her window as her husband relayed the message that she couldn't talk with me. He said it was still impossible for her to discuss the tragedy without getting extremely upset.

A man, however, who had been Hugh's roommate when he shot Professor Sweat, relayed a strange story by phone. After he graduated at the orphanage, he attended a university in Raleigh where the state prison was also located. He had made a delivery close by and was unloading a truck when he heard someone call his name. He looked up at a prison window and, to his utter amazement, he saw Hugh. When he got over the shock of this weird coincidence, he asked him how he was doing. Hugh, looking extremely pale and sad, responded, "I'm okay, but no one should ever have to live in a place like this." I've asked myself how someone who we respected and sincerely liked had come to that. But, knowing the details of his life, perhaps it is not so difficult to understand, which would be true of his partner in the crime, also.

I've wondered, often what became of Hugh and Billy Ray, but when a reporter tried to locate them in 2000 in the prison system, officials had no record of either one. I tried to get information on the North Carolina Department of Corrections' website and also failed to find any data on them. It seemed to me that they had been completely erased from official memory.

There have been many rumors through the years about them including one that Billy Ray had gotten into a fight with another prisoner and had been killed. This is easy to believe because of his temper and his penchant for fighting. Others say that Hugh was released and went to California, where he later died. Someone had seen an obituary that described a man who could definitely have been him since his brother lived in that state. Although I doubt that we will ever know their actual fate, I do hope both found some forgiveness for what they did as teenagers.

I often ask myself if the murders could have been prevented. Billy Ray and Hugh had experienced violence and heartbreaking disappointment their entire lives. Professor Sweat had dedicated his life to children and although he was what appeared to a child to be arrogant, he did not deserve to be murdered. The young boy, Wade, was just too close when that explosion of pent-up rage caused these boys to exact revenge for all the wrongs which they felt they had suffered. I know there were many lessons to be learned from the murders; instead people chose not to deal with it, and that was harmful too.

Momma was determined to take us out of the home as soon as possible, but it was a long and difficult eight months later when she was finally able to rent a house and we left the orphanage. I was relieved to leave that place far behind, and I realized we were luckier than the children who had to remain. My siblings and I didn't discuss the murders until many years later.

Today, when I hear about grief counselors being brought in for children after people are killed, I am extremely thankful. I remember the awful silence on our campus in 1951 and its effect on us. I know now that we paid a terrible price by burying dark memories within; this can sometimes destroy a chance for happiness. I learned later that another murder, a student killing a student, had taken place in the orphanage not long before we arrived there. I wondered too if a heavy silence closed in around the campus then too. Did anyone discover the real reasons behind the murder then? If Hugh and Billy Ray had been able to express the pain they experienced during their young lives with a professional, often it's possible these tragic events may never have happened. These two boys were quite different, but it was pain turned into rage that brought them together and ruined so many lives.

I know that some of the emotional turmoil in our lives could have been prevented if there were a few adults who were able to comfort us. I've had to forgive them, because I now realize they were not able to help. Many years later, however, I found peace by facing these memories and through a great deal of forgiveness. I forgave myself first, and then all the other players in this dark event that was woven so deeply into the very fabric of my childhood. I'm grateful I found the courage to face those ghosts and release the pain surrounding my time in the orphanage.

I'm especially thankful for the forgiveness I found for myself because I know that forgiveness is the key to loving ourselves. I sincerely hope that all of the children from The Home for Motherless Children who lived through the murders, the loss of loved ones and the forced silence, have found peace. This includes Hugh and Billy Ray. I know forgiveness is possible even for them. I sincerely hope peace is too.

# Where Did All the Flowers Go?

Spring didn't come to the foothills that year
For on a cold and lonely winter's night
A dark and frightful thing happened here
Then those we loved were dead or full of fear
In this place for homeless children so dear
And we wouldn't see Spring soon, it was clear.

We would not see the dogwood's bloom near
Nor the pretty pink azaleas' color dear
For the children it was such a dreary year.
Why did the pretty flowers go away from here?
Although some did not shed a tear
The children wondered why joy did disappear.

So much sadness, perhaps we didn't see or hear
Spring arrive in the Appalachian hills so near
For each child was infected with a dreadful fear
So Spring didn't come for us that year
But in time Summer rains washed away our tears
And Spring returned after many, many years.

*Judy H James*

# Forgiveness

Forgiveness is the
key
To loving myself and
Loving myself the path
To loving others
Without forgiveness I remain
Locked within an angry heart
Forgiveness
Opens the portals that lead
To the freedom I seek
For it pries open the windows
Of my soul
And guides me softly through
The door to love
And to joy.

# Misty Mountain Morn

It's a blue, misty mountain morn
It is mysterious yet so warm all around
Mountains surrounded and by a soft, mist adorned
Enveloping me so completely that I can hear no sounds
It's here in my mind that earth does
end and heaven abounds.

# A Stranger,
# an Angel

I've always felt that I have had angels watching over me; they show up when needed and bring miracles into my life. When I was a child it was unreasonable for me to even dream of going to college, but I decided I was going quite early in life. I had no way of financing four years' tuition for what seemed like an outrageous amount, since I had no money and no one in my immediate environment who could assist me. Everyone except Momma said I should get married, have babies—like most girls did in the South—and forget about college. However, I was determined to get at least a four-year degree in order to climb out of the poverty that had made life difficult for my family. Poverty was a big factor in molding my life and I'm now grateful for the lessons it brought me. Yet, I knew even then that I wanted to experience luxury too. Momma taught me that education was the golden gate leading to all my dreams and she strongly supported my absolute intention to go to college.

In high school, I was a leader in my class, but had only a solid B average and that didn't justify a scholarship in those days (1956). I did, however, have two strong supporters: my principal, Mr. Womack, and the superintendent. To my surprise, Mr. Bryan, the Superintendent of Schools, had graduated from high school at the orphanage where we had lived for a few years. He was aware of the tragedy which occurred while we were there and from the moment we arrived at Central High School, he had shown a special interest in my siblings and me. Both men recommended that I contact the organization sponsored by the local cotton mills. The group loaned money for college to the children of their workers, who would pay it back after graduation. They assisted with the application and because of their positive references, I was successful in getting a loan to start each year for four years, as long as my grades were up to par.

In college, I also worked several jobs and the money went directly toward my tuition. My sophomore year at a junior college, I had two jobs: one in the student union and the other as an assistant to a history professor. I really enjoyed working with this professor who had been

*Judy H James*

very helpful to me. However, sadly he died of bone cancer in the middle of that year. It was difficult for all of us to lose this teacher who was loved by faculty and students alike. His death also substantially reduced my income since the assistant's position no longer existed. This caused a very real problem because without that income, I couldn't pay the rest of my tuition or my room and board. This meant I couldn't eat in the cafeteria and didn't have the money to buy food, either. Although Momma sent a lot of peanut butter and crackers, she couldn't provide any cash for my expenses. My friends in the dorm were extremely sympathetic and helped all they could by scrounging food for me, such as toast and jelly or anything else they could sneak out of the cafeteria. We laughed a lot and it was fun for a while, but I was not eating well and was afraid that my skin might turn peanut-butter brown since I had eaten so much of the stuff.

I knew I had to do something soon but couldn't imagine where to start since I'd already borrowed money from every source I knew. The school had notified me that I would not be allowed to attend classes unless the rest of my tuition was paid. Surprisingly, they had not kicked me out of the dorm yet, although that was looming over my head also. I was still absolutely determined to graduate but was aware that time was running out. Then, much to my surprise, Momma wrote with the news that Mr. Womack, who had heard of my predicament, had given her the name of a man who might help. He owned several cotton mills in a nearby town and was known to assist college students who he felt deserved it. He did, however, require that you come to his home and go to dinner with him—at which time he would interview you. He would then make his decision based on his impression during this time with you. Although I was extremely nervous, I called and set up the interview as soon as possible.

I didn't have nice clothes, so my dormmates loaned me an outfit and helped me get ready for the interview. A friend drove me to the man's home and dropped me off in his driveway. I found myself alone looking at a large mansion and feeling small and insignificant. I knew poor very well, but this definitely looked like rich to me and I was not familiar with it. At nineteen years old I had never been around wealthy people and was scared out of my mind. I was a college kid going to see a wealthy man that I'd never met, who didn't know me and I had to ask him for what seemed to me like a huge amount of money. I knew I had no option but to go through with this or pack up my suitcase of dreams and go home.

I walked to the huge door and rang the bell, knowing that this night and this interview could determine my future, or at least delay it by forcing me to drop out of school. The idea of having to drop out was worse than the fear of the interview, so I decided it was necessary for me to buck up, handle my nerves and perform at my best.

I don't remember much about the interview except it was in an expensive restaurant, which unnerved me. Having never been to an exceptionally nice restaurant, I didn't know which of all those silver forks by my plate to use first. Thank goodness, the man was an extremely nice person who did everything he could to put me at ease. This helped me relax and answer his questions, while, I hoped, eating with the correct fork instead of looking like the young hillbilly that I was.

It was quite an evening and a learning experience for me; yet I must have performed adequately. Soon, I received a letter stating he was glad to assist me. It also contained a sizable check which was enough to cover all my expenses for the year. I cried tears of joy knowing I was now able to finish my sophomore year and move forward. My dorm friends celebrated with me and Momma came to join us. It was the only time in my four years she was able to visit me except for graduation when, as Momma often said, "I'll be there with bells on!" Momma knew the generous support my friends had provided and, to my absolute amazement, she brought her famous hot dogs, chili and slaw, as well as banana pudding for all. We had a lot of fun that day and we gulped down the delicious homemade meal in the midst of a mighty celebration. I don't know how Momma could afford that meal

*Judy H James*

or transportation there, since we never had a car in the family, but it was the best meal I've ever had. I'll never forget that special day with Momma and my friends. I was extremely happy knowing I didn't have to go home feeling like a failure. I knew people would again start that old Southern chant for all unmarried girls over 15 years old: "You don't need no education, you're jus' gonna wind up getting married and having babies." Thank goodness I escaped going through that maddening experience again.

I wrote my generous benefactor a thank-you note immediately and told him I would repay the money after college. His response was: "I don't want to be paid back, but I would ask that when you can, please pass it on to someone who needs assistance." I've always remembered that and have helped students, financially and in other ways. Although I never saw the man again, I often think of him, even now, sixty years later. I'm very grateful for this "angel" who appeared in my life when I truly needed one. I was a stranger to him and yet he was willing to give me money for my education without any strings attached. Without a doubt, it felt like a miracle to me and I accepted it as one. This was a pivotal event in my life. I knew then that I would finish college regardless of what obstacles might show up along my way.

When I went to Wake Forest University it was much more expensive, and I've often wondered how the tuition was paid. I worked many jobs, including delivering papers before classes each day, but they paid very little. I did have one small scholarship at the university, but the money including my annual loan, the job income, and scholarship did not ever add up to the tuition. Despite this, I never had any difficulty with college expenses again and it's still a mystery. I assume angels are watching over me and they've shown up in many shapes and sizes; sometimes without my being aware of them. Momma taught me to believe that things always work out for the best and I continue to believe this. I know that just holding this belief is very powerful.

Many angels have supported me along the way and I graduated with a very good education (including which is the correct fork for the right time). I also learned a lot of good, common sense from Momma, which I believe is more valuable than a college education. I'm very thankful for my angels, especially the stranger who paid my tuition that year when I was desperate. This taught me never to doubt that there are many good people and to be there for others when possible. I gained unforgettable lessons from a generous stranger with an open heart. And like him, I believe we have an obligation to pass it on to others.

I shall always be grateful to him for his unselfish act of love. Thinking of my experience with this gentleman-angel has always strengthened my belief in the inherent goodness of people.

# *Love*

Love is at the heart
Of all Creation
For God is Love
And when we have
Loved others
We have loved God
And to love
Is to be Godlike.

# A

# Long-Lost

# Brother

We did not find our long, lost brother until he was about seventy years old

My father, the wandering man (like Johnny Appleseed) spread his seed far and wide as he moved around the country. He clearly thought of himself as a genuine Casanova, and I doubt even he knew how many children he actually had. As he wandered, we children were always left behind with Momma. Thank goodness, for if we had gone with him, we would have wound up stranded on the side of a road, with no prospects whatsoever. However, to be honest, he did not invite us to go along but once, when the law was on his back, and then within a few days of reaching our destination he dumped us. Daddy put the five of us (four children and Momma) on a bus, almost penniless, to parts unknown, and I'm sure he breathed a sigh of relief, since he had a girlfriend waiting in the wings.

His mode of operation, I repeat, was to show up occasionally and promise us our dream life with our own home. He'd stay about a week, but by then he was miserable and off he'd go like a shadow in the night. I never knew why he returned so many times, so eventually I assumed some woman had thrown him out and he came to us for R&R after his latest adventure. He'd arrive, as if he were a wandering bard making his rounds of the villages and regale us with wild stories. He always laughed at his own jokes with the same odd laugh. It rumbled up from his stomach, causing his shoulders to bounce up and down and then emerge as deep-throated chuckles, topped off with a one-sided grin. However, it was laughter that never achieved any joy whatsoever. It seemed to be something he did automatically, perhaps as a way to clue us in on when to laugh which was often necessary.

Sometimes when he was gone for an extended period, I'd ask my mother, "Momma, do you think Daddy is dead?" She would invariably reply, without a trace of bitterness, "Lordy no, honey, only the good die young." Considering his wandering, amorous ways, it's possible he spawned kids all over the country, which means I could have brothers and sisters up and down this great continent. Now, that thought could make a soul start wondering how many brothers and sisters she may have, as well as when they might show up at the door. I've never had anyone ask me how many siblings I have, when I didn't stop to think and then question how many to reveal or how complicated an explanation I should offer. Since Momma also had a child by a first marriage, my answer usually is on the order of: "I think I have eight brothers and sisters, but I may have more." This reply has revitalized many boring conversations.

When I was about sixty-two years old and Daddy had recently died, we found our half-brother, James. He lived surprisingly close, in another small Southern town in North Carolina. Jim was about seventy-three years old and a retired veterinarian. I only regret I did not meet him earlier. He was one of the apples that fell from Dad's tree and he rates as "golden delicious."

My long-lost brother seems exactly like Daddy, but he could also be described as not like him at all. He tells jokes and laughs at them, has Daddy's gift of gab, looks like him—with the same mannerisms, the same bald pattern—and has both his charm and his hot temper. Jim is a wonderful man, though, and an honest comparison of father and son shows: Daddy was totally irresponsible, and Jim is very responsible; Daddy was cynical and Jim optimistic; Daddy was paranoid and suspicious, and Jim likes and trusts people; Daddy was dishonest to his very core, and Jim is an honest, churchgoing man. Also, as I've said, Daddy was a restless, wandering bard. Jim lived in his hometown in the North Carolina foothills as a child and is still there today and will probably die there. He has been married to the same great lady for many years. Most important, Daddy was a lousy father to all the children he sired and Jim's a good father. One of the great mysteries of my life is how these two men could be so much alike and yet be true opposites.

Some of dad's many children get together several times a year and we half expect a perfect stranger to knock on the door and proclaim he is one of his offspring. Short of a DNA test, we'd never know for sure. Considering our positive experience with Jim, we'd probably accept him without question into our expanding Scotch/Irish clan. Then we would hear his story and have a good laugh about our odd family tree.

We four children, as I have said, were raised by a loving, determined mother and had a tough time, but a strong family bond got us through the difficult times. We moved too many times throughout the South, running from the poverty that always seemed to track us down. We lived with relatives more often than the relatives or we even care to remember, and in the orphanage. However, after the murders at the orphanage, with no assistance from our wandering daddy, Momma was finally able to rent a place and we were thrilled to be together in our own house at last. It was a small mill-hill house with holes in the floor, sunlight beaming through the wallboards and the bathroom on the back porch. It was our first real home, the single-family house we had dreamed of for years. Only love and orphanage time, plus a lot of living in other people's homes, could have made that ramshackle house look like a little mansion to us. After years of being separated, we were together for our last years of school in that small, Southern, conservative town nestled in the shadows of the mountains. We soon discovered Daddy had three other children in the same county and eventually we learned about our older brother, Jim. Momma encouraged us to contact him, so when Daddy died we decided it was time and we began to make phone calls.

Through these inquiries, we located our mysterious older brother, about whom we had only heard rumors. We invited him to come to the funeral, but he insisted he did not want to intrude on our grief. Little did he know … for I can't honestly say we grieved at Dad's funeral. There probably was more forgiving Daddy than grieving for him. Any grief was for what might have been and how much Daddy had missed by walking away from his children and wives. Perhaps we grieved a little too, about the high cost of the funeral for which we four siblings had agreed to fork up the money.

After the funeral our newly discovered half-sibling, Jim came to my sister's house and we all met for the first time. We siblings told stories of our childhood, laughed, cried, then laughed and cried some more, and we bonded. Our families were there too and it was an exciting and emotional time for everyone. We met their children and they met ours; cousins met cousins and aunts and uncles introduced each other to nieces and nephews. The similarities of the two groups who had never met before were amazing. It was a little strange to meet a brother for the first time when he's seventy-three years old and you're in your sixties, but with open hearts it can be wonderful. Momma was present for the reunion and was happy that we had cleared up the story of our older brother. She knew this was a necessary part of our coming to terms with Daddy's rejection. We learned we weren't the only ones who had experienced it and we all had survived as seemingly normal.

Talking with Jim, we learned our childhood was very different from his, although he had a loving and supportive mother too. In contrast to our family, Jim was his mother's only child. She raised him with the assistance of his maternal grandparents, but he had always wondered why his father had abandoned him and never returned, as he did with us. Oddly enough, Jim was about seventy years old before he met Daddy, when he visited him in a nursing home, and he still questions why his father never returned to see him. His new siblings assured him that he got the best of the deal, rather than having to contend with Daddy's broken promises and his secret, nocturnal escapes.

Jim was obviously loved and cared for by his mother's family, yet he had always wanted brothers and sisters. No one told him that his five sisters and two brothers lived within forty miles of his home. There is certainly irony in the fact that most of his life, Jim said he often felt lonely and yearned for a large family. To more normal families, it may seem weird finding a brother when he's seventy-three years old. However, it's better than crossing to that other realm without ever getting acquainted with the guy we call our long-lost brother, Jim. The story has a happy ending, for we loved our new brother and his wife,

*Judy H James*

and we often get together to talk and enjoy each other as if we were a normal family.

Daddy left us a wonderful Scotch/Irish legacy: we all love to share stories and jokes. We laugh a lot and Jim has a wonderful laugh which ripples with joy. Very little of our time at family reunions has been spent discussing Daddy, which I choose to believe indicates that we have forgiven him. I do often wonder how much wandering he is allowed in the other realm now. He's probably resting, however, after his years of rolling around the country searching for something which proved so elusive to him in this life. All of his children who I have met thus far say, "May he rest in peace.

Our long lost brother, Jim passed away in 2005 and we miss him very much. We still visit with his widow who has given permission to use his poem.

# Bird Talk

Late in the yard
Picking up trash
I heard a bird's voice
A wee bit rash.

Looking up
I saw it was she
Her voice too soft
Knew it couldn't be a he.

She said to me
"You're too close to my nest
And the place I'll soon
Be building my nest."

"I'm sorry," I said
"I'll move away
And visit you again
Another day."


Jim Hughey

# Love and Joy

Once upon a time
When I dwelled among the stars
And I danced with angels
I discovered Love and Joy
As my purpose in life
I felt this in my heart
And I wrote it upon my soul
Therefore
When I have loved and laughed
For many, many moons
Upon this earth
Then I shall return
To take my place
Among the stars
And with the angels
I shall reside in the arms of God
The arms of Love
For eternity.

Aunt Ed returning
from her service
in the WACs

With Max and Iris
Hughey 1945

Judy Hughey
Engagement Picture
1960

President of The League of Women Voters, Judy
welcomes a federal judge and two circuit judges.

# Remembering Momma

# and Her Near-Death Experience

Momma went to "heaven" and talked with God but she decided to come back home for awhile.

Momma died and went to "heaven," but she came back to love us for a little longer and a lot better. She certainly hadn't been a saint before, but after her "near-death" experience, Momma became almost angelic. For eighty-nine years prior to her heavenly visit, she had been loving, strong, sassy, opinionated, as well as harsh in her criticism, and despite this she was loved by many. She was a simple, uneducated woman who was actually a complicated and fascinating person. She was the center of the universe for her children and grandchildren, so we were ecstatic when she returned to us from that other realm. She told us she decided to return, and I believe God allowed her to make that decision. Momma lived only a matter of months after this divine experience and that time was spent preparing for her return. There were things she definitely needed to clean up before she returned to God's country, permanently.

Momma did not treat my older sister, Iris, with respect even when she was an adult. I recall the time Iris came to the house after a hair salon appointment. With excitement in her voice, she asked Momma how she liked her new hairdo. In a heartbeat, Momma replied, "Well, I hope you didn't pay someone to do that to you." As a child, I remember my Momma as someone I could never quite reach. I was constantly trying to get her approval or hoping she would hold me and say she loved me. Momma had always been someone who everyone in the family respected for her old-fashioned wisdom and the sacrifices she made for us. But she was like her momma in many ways, though, for despite loving us unconditionally, she was not nurturing toward some of her children. I tried very much to please Momma and I worked hard, was a leader in school, but I felt it was never good enough. She never held me like she did my baby sister, nor did she seem to care for me as she did my younger brother, Max. However, Momma's own experiences with love and nurturing from birth had been disastrous. Her mother rejected her cruelly, her father passively, and her husbands, repeatedly. As a child, though, I was not aware of all of this and I didn't understand why she seemed distant to me.

Momma was a strong Southern matriarch to whom family was everything. She often said: "Blood is thicker than water and don't ever forget it." Daddy left the family when we were young, and returned all too often for me, but never stayed around long. Since he had never taken responsibility for us or any of his other children, she was the only one on whom we could depend. Momma worked in a cotton mill to support us until she had an accident there in which her hand was cut badly. As I've said, then we children were constantly dropped off to live with various relatives and other places less pleasant, which naturally caused Momma a lot of pain. These times of separation were always difficult for us too, yet there was one constant in our life that gave us hope and that was Momma's fierce determination to have us together. She came to our rescue many times, so we knew she would return for us as soon as possible. This was especially true when we were in the orphanage and the murders took place. After this horrible event, Momma was determined to get us out of there as soon as possible. It took a while but eventually, she was able to come for us. Although the house she rented was little more than a shack, it was a real stand-alone home and a mansion to us. It was also the first time we had all been together in years.

We were poor, but Momma was proud and did not allow us to feel sorry for ourselves. She had a way of letting us know that we were better than our surroundings, which were often pathetic. She gave us wonderful beliefs and constantly told us: "You can do anything you want to, if you want it bad enough and you work hard." Momma would not allow us to say "I can't" to anything we were required to do. If she asked us to do something and we actually got up the nerve to say that, she'd reply emphatically, "No, 'can't' never could do nothin'. Get up from there and do what I said and don't ever let me hear you say that word again."

Momma had gone to school only till the sixth grade, and had to quit during the Depression to work at the mill to help support the family. Each time she got a pay check she was allowed to keep only the change in it for herself - no matter how small it was. She insisted we get an education because she thought it was the proven path to prosperity heaven. She wanted us to have the good life but above everything else, she expected us to behave ourselves and be honest in everything we did. In her handwritten will, which we found after her death, she stated that she was satisfied with her life because, "My children turned out to be good, honest people and that's all I could ask for." Momma believed in the Norman Rockwell America of Franklin D. Roosevelt, her hero. Like him, she had a knack for making anything seem within reach. She believed that with sheer determination and a positive attitude, nothing was impossible. And she expected us to go out into the world and prove it.

We were raised in the 1940s and '50s, when it was a disgrace to be from a divorced family. Momma told us, "Always remember, you're just as good as anybody, but no better than anyone else." She was a dyed-in-the-wool Southerner, but she never treated the blacks around us the way others in the South did. We lived in several conservative mill towns, but all prejudice stopped at our front door because she would not allow it to step across her doorstep. Momma's childhood rejection and her position as the community's divorced woman was the fuel that fed her compassion and, indirectly, ours too. Families of divorce were sometimes thought to be outside polite society in those days, so to be completely accepted she knew we needed to do well in school, go to church and work hard to earn respect. Much of this was never spoken, yet we knew how she felt because she constantly encouraged us to do our best.

Momma was different from most of our neighbors, for although she was a good woman, she didn't attend church. She did, however, recognize the extreme importance of the church in small Southern towns. She religiously saw to it that we were dressed and in Sunday school every week at the local Baptist church, wherever we lived. Momma stayed home, rested and worshipped in her own way. She worked at home on that day, but as she said, it was a labor of love. It was her only time away from the bone-tiring job in the cotton mill, which she was forced to return to despite her disfigured hand; it was the only way she could make a half-decent living. She wasn't about to give up her sacred day of rest, even under old-fashioned religious pressure. Once when the preacher visited her and insisted, "Mrs. Hughey, we certainly would like to see you on Sundays." Without hesitation, Momma replied, "Well, Preacher, I'll be right here, and I'd be more than glad to have you visit."

Although Momma might have had some shortcomings as a mother, she was a wonderful grandmother and her grandchildren absolutely adored her and liked spending time with her. Momma loved gospel music, especially Elvis Presley's, and often listened to it with them. Once when she was staying in our home, a local Baptist minister knocked on the door and my daughter, Abby, opened it. The minister asked if her mother was home and she told him I was not. (I was listening nearby but did not venture out, deciding to let the child handle the questions.) She told him her 'grammy' was there with her. "Well, honey, does your 'grammy' take you to Sunday school each Sunday?" he asked. Abby, who was only about seven years old, proudly announced, "No, but we listen to Elvis Presley's gospel music every Sunday morning."

When Momma was in her eighties, she had a heart attack and almost passed away in the ambulance. The doctor said she was in critical condition, so we rushed home to North Carolina. When my sister Becky arrived, she was shocked. Momma's body was so riddled with needles and medical contraptions that she couldn't talk. However, as Becky came into her hospital room, Momma immediately began frantically trying to tell her something. My sister was sure Momma was in terrible pain, but when asked, Momma shook her head "No." Desperate, Becky gave her a pencil and paper, and she wrote, "Bring me my makeup right now." She put on her makeup and immediately began to improve. Like any self-respecting Southern lady, Momma didn't go outside her home without makeup - looking her best - and she was not about to change, heart attack or not.

Momma got better and was as sassy and independent as always. She was determined to live alone and even refused a medical monitor in case of emergencies. However, a few years later she fell in the middle of the night and lay on the floor, semiconscious, for many hours. She never quite recovered from that night and eventually had to go into a nursing home. Soon afterwards, Momma became seriously ill and lapsed into a deep coma. She was unconscious for what seemed like an eternity to us, but it was only about three days. We didn't think she could possibly survive the serious emotional and physical trauma she had suffered, and we were distraught at the thought of losing her.

As we often did, we underestimated Momma's strength and determination. My sister and I were present and experienced her unbelievable joy when she awoke from the coma. On awakening, Momma took in her surroundings and was obviously surprised. Then, staring back and forth at the two of us for a few seconds, she waved her arms above her head while shouting, "Judy, Becky, it's you—I'm alive, I'm alive, hallelujah, I'm alive!" Momma was like a sinner at an old-time revival, who was shouting with relief and joy for having been born again. She had gone to "heaven" and stood in the presence of God's love. It was a dramatic, life-changing experience that brought a real transformation in her.

Momma told us she had talked with her parents and relatives on the other side and, amazingly, she also had talked with her children who were still living. After these talks with all her important kinfolk, she decided she needed to return. Although she would never say why, this became obvious in the following days. As she told her heavenly story, someone asked if she had talked with the Lord, and she responded that she had. When asked what they had talked about, she stated emphatically, "That is between me and my Lord, and nobody's business." She was right. We never asked again, knowing it would be useless. At times, I wanted to discuss her rare experience with her, but she was not completely in the earthly realm, seeming to have one foot on the other side. Also, when

I was with her I just wanted to sit and enjoy her loving presence, which I had not experienced before.

Momma's personality and her face were transformed after her divine visit. Her features softened, she appeared serene and there was a soft light that seemed to rest on her. I noted a complete change in her critical nature and she no longer gossiped about neighbors and family. Momma was bedridden during this period, and Becky took her from an unpleasant nursing home to her house to care for her. Becky is really to be commended, for it was a huge job to prepare for Momma's care and it took time and money. Even though she had some financial help, her job was not easy. She rented a special bed, which she had to put in her dining room, and also other medical equipment, as well as a nurse to come in each week. Originally, this didn't seem wise to me because Momma needed medical care and I thought she would make a difficult patient since she had always been fiercely independent.

As it turned out, Momma loved being cared for by her daughter and son-in-law, Red, and it was a blessing for everyone. Becky even learned to give her insulin shots, and taught me also. I hated needles because of the many shots when I had been ill, but I learned and gave her the shots occasionally. Momma never complained. She gracefully welcomed our help and this was the greatest gift she had ever given us, for it had been difficult, previously, for Momma to accept any assistance. Becky did a great job. It became obvious that when you are guided by love, nothing is impossible, and things are made easier.

It appeared that Momma had returned to make things right in her life. She'd had a favorite brother that she loved although he was an alcoholic and died all too early. She requested to see his widow who Grandma had blamed for all of his problems as the old "blood is thicker..." belief ran strong in our clan. As usual, the entire family followed Grandma's lead in this, and for many years my aunt suffered under this unfair and really spiteful blame. Momma knew it was time to ask forgiveness for her part in this hateful behavior, which had been a deep wound within the family for too long. They talked, things were made right between the two of them and a healing took place in the family.

Like her momma before her, Momma had her favorite children. My sister Iris was not one of those cherished and she was given too much responsibility as the oldest girl. When we were young, Momma took out her frustrations on her and would whip her so severely that sometimes I would have to stop her. Iris probably reminded her of our wayward daddy, who she missed very much when he was off wandering—which was most of the time. Despite this, Iris loved her and unselfishly visited and assisted Momma for many years. After the "near-death" experience, we could even see a change in Momma's attitude toward her oldest daughter and they were able to talk. Though I could see their relationship improve, Iris has had to work hard to forgive Momma for all those years of mistreatment.

Momma stayed here on earth with us for a while after her visit to the other side and during that time she was loving and warm. She always had been special in the extended family, and relatives who visited her bedside found it easy to express their affection. She had a wonderful presence, and I finally felt the acceptance from her that I had wanted so much. Momma had always been like a butterfly to me -colorful and inspiring, but quite elusive. When I was an adult, she wrote to me to say she was proud of me and my work with children. But even then, she was unable to express her love. During this short period with her before her death, I could feel her love and there was no need for words. I'll always be extremely grateful for this lovely, sweet time with Momma.

Momma's way of seeing the light and learning to love better may not have been the easy way, but it was short, affective and transformative. It only took her about three days in a coma, during which time she had a glimpse of the Divine. Whatever she and her Lord discussed, it was such a powerful experience that it changed Momma. In my years of searching for more of a connection to my Creator, I am often envious of her fabulous, quick sojourn with God. The next time God sent the angels to get Momma, she went willingly because she had made things right on earth and she was not afraid. She returned to heaven in 2003, and I know she is still with me and her family in spirit. I talk with Momma now and I have a better relationship with her since she went to heaven than when on earth, for she rarely talks back.

Often, I have daydreamed about Momma, there in that heavenly realm, talking to white-robed relatives, especially her Momma who had never shown her love. Since that realm is a place of loving kindness, I imagine that Grandma is sweet and affectionate to Momma. She is able to sit on her poppa's lap too. In my dreams, I see Momma talking with Hal (my half-brother who Grandma had taken) and explaining there in that place of warmth and light how much she had always wanted him with her. She also tells him why she could not bring him home. They talk for the first time of his pain and her heartbreak, and her terrible regrets about his life. I see him forgiving her and then Grandma as well for holding on to him rather than letting him be a part of the family he loved and yearned for. I believe Momma forgives herself also for not fighting Grandma for her son. In this daydream, I envision these sessions bringing Momma a peace she had not experienced in her earthly life.

I wonder why God chose to give Momma this unusual opportunity before she passed over permanently. Perhaps it was because she missed out on love in her life, yet kept a positive spirit without giving in to self-pity. How fortunate she was to be able to visit "heaven" for a moment and have this unique experience. We each might wish to visit the other side, have a talk with God, perhaps receive divine understanding and then be gifted with the time to prepare for the heavenly life. Momma was a special lady who sacrificed greatly for her family, but I believe we each can have great spiritual experiences too, if we are open to them.

I know Momma made her own decision to return home. She needed to find forgiveness, to finally open her heart completely and to show us that special love. Whatever the explanation for Momma's "near-death"

*Judy H James*

experience, I thank God for the wonderful gift she received. This demonstrated again for me that love is the most powerful force on earth. I believe love transported Momma on that heavenly ride and it was love which drove her back home to us. I was then able to see her in a different light - as the person she truly was - and to understand her better. To stand in my Momma's presence and for the first time to feel cherished, accepted and at peace was a true gift which I am unable to adequately describe. During these days with her, I felt I was standing in the presence of her love and God's love. I shall forever be grateful for that lovely time with Momma, for it had a profound influence on me. It was a time of much forgiveness and love.

# Loving Better

I wish I had loved you better, Momma
We could've ridden the rainbows, you and I
And found our joy together.

I wish I had loved you better, Daddy
We could've blown in the wind to exotic places
And gotten to know each other.

I wish I'd loved you better, brothers & sisters
We could have flown into the deep, blue skies
And found lovely dreams together.

I wish I had loved you better, dear husband
We could've shone bright as the stars at night
And found peace & happiness together.

I wish I had loved you better, my children
We could have swung on shiny moonbeams
And been there in joy for each other.

I wish I had loved me better, too
But now we can find our happiness together
For we can love each other so much better.

# Death

Why do we fear your coming?
We don't actually know you
So do you even exist?

Death
Are you only a mystical passage
From one life to another
Spiritually, do you even exist?

Death
Why do those who passed over
Saw the light and returned
Have no fear if you do exist?

Death
Could we come to love you
Simply accept and have no fear
Even when you are very near?

Judy and Momma
at her grandson's
wedding

1994

(Momma)

Florence Devine
Hughey

1999

*Judy H James*

# What a Relief

# and

# Freedom!

My discovery and release of a traumatic childhood experience and what followed is like a miracle to me. I finally realized why I felt extremely lonely each night when trying to fall asleep. The loneliness was connected to an event that occurred when I was about seven years old and had just been diagnosed with rheumatic fever. The doctor recommended that I go to the University Hospital in Richmond, about 100 miles away from home. Again, since Momma couldn't afford it, the Virginia Department of Health would pay for it.

Momma and I arrived at the hospital after a long bus trip, late in the evening when it was dark. After I was admitted, the nurse led us to the ward where there were other children who were already sleeping. She put me in a bed and I can still hear the clanging of hard, cold metal against metal as the nurse pulled the rails up on the sides of the bed— and that terrible feeling of being trapped.

Momma began saying goodbye, and I could feel the loneliness creeping in on me even before she was gone; I knew I would not see her again for a very long time. She didn't hug or comfort me at all because it was not her way - or at least not with me. Momma once told me she thought I didn't need to be held or comforted because I was independent and could take care of myself. But I was only seven and, like any child, I wanted her to show me love. That night I needed it desperately. I could not cry out for her to take me with her because I was told to be absolutely quiet so as not to wake the other sick children in the room. I knew if I cried, it would upset Momma too, so I was trying to be strong. Then the nurse turned off the light and my last sight of Momma leaving was her shadowy silhouette in the open door, made by the hall light in front of her. The door closed and I was literally screaming inside, pleading for her to come back for me; but I held that silent scream deep within. I felt completely alone and the darkness engulfed me as an overwhelming loneliness settled in on me. Fear gripped my heart too, for I wasn't sure, at that moment, that anyone cared enough to ever return and take me home. This was not the first time I had felt abandoned, nor was it the last, but it was the most painful.

I was in the hospital for about three months, and no one in my family was able to visit since Momma had to work and couldn't afford it. Daddy, as usual, was in some unknown place, and I was not sure if he knew or cared that I was in the hospital. His brother, Uncle Marvin, who I hadn't known before lived nearby, and his family came to see me occasionally. They also drove me home when I was released since it was difficult for Momma to come. While I was there, the doctors and nurses who knew Momma couldn't visit were very loving and my days were pleasant (aside from the hundreds of needles puncturing me). Each night, however, as the lights were turned off, the dark loneliness returned.

For many years afterward, when falling asleep I felt lonely, with tremendous discomfort around my heart, and I didn't know why. I wasn't afraid of the dark, but I dreaded dealing with that nocturnal demon which always came before sleep finally descended upon me. Each time I awoke for any reason, I again fought that unrelenting loneliness. Meditation helped chase it away temporarily, but it still returned to haunt me. I yearned to rid myself of it forever, so that I could lie down to sleep and welcome the lovely night as a time of rest. I had never discussed this with anyone; I was ashamed because it seemed to me that it was a weakness. Peace didn't come for a long time, however, because I had pushed that sad event deep inside, almost beyond memory.

One evening while wrestling with the loneliness, I remembered that unhappy hospital night and how painful it had been. Then I became aware of the connection, for the first time, with my nighttime feelings of abandonment, and understood how it had begun. Just the awareness helped me release much of the pain around that time. My final relief came when I was able to forgive Momma for leaving me in that dark room without showing me her love. I realized how upset she must have been that night, having to leave her child there in a dark hospital room and take the long bus trip home, alone. She couldn't show her sadness, perhaps for the same reason I could not cry. She was afraid it would upset me and I began to see that she too had felt terrible. I imagined she must have sat down somewhere after leaving me and cried her heart out. Finally, I also came to accept that she cared more than she was ever able to show me. I had thought most of my life that she didn't love me enough to be upset about leaving me. It was wonderful to realize her love and although she had died a few years before, I was able to understand this event and the effect it must have had on her too.

The nightly discomfort left me. I will never forget that first wonderful evening when I lay down to sleep and the loneliness demon didn't come to visit. Instead, my visitor was indescribable joy, and each night I savor this feeling and the peace that comes with it. Now I do not need television or anything as I fall asleep; instead, I accept this time as an opportunity to meditate, to compose poetry or to gain more acceptance of my interesting childhood. I forgave Momma for leaving me alone those many times, by putting myself in her place and feeling her despair. I am eternally grateful that I was able to free myself from the sharp emotions which came stabbing at my heart every night for many years. Oh, what a relief it is to experience the freedom from that sad memory!

I am convinced that for true happiness to occur, we must always keep searching deep within, and release those negative memories which we have buried in our subconscious that cause us misery. Until we free our self from this body of pain, we cannot be at peace or be our true self. The process of freeing ourselves of negative baggage may be difficult for a moment or two, but it brings relief and joy into our life. This releasing of painful memories has often brought me surprises, and in the end it is always a positive, life-changing experience for which I am eternally grateful. Forgiveness is vital in this process. It brings self - love which is extremely important for it is then that we are capable of a real love for others. Love is powerful and can cross over all boundaries. Even though Momma is in another realm, I felt her presence and her love during this time of healing. She was near and comforting to me.

# Present Always

My dear one

I'm here for you

With calm understanding

I'll be present too

Though we may be separated

Those we love live in our hearts

And we're never far apart

I can feel your pain

And know your joy

So, like the summer rain

And its many showers

I'll be there bringing flowers.

So, my dear friend

On this you can depend

In every way I'm here for you

Present, patient and loving too.

# A Sweet Peace

There is a sweet peace which
Having not attained it
Is beyond
All understanding.
Having once attained this peace
There is no need to understand
For your heart and soul
Always know and feel it.

# Life,

# Love,

# and

# Marriage

Jerry and I loved each other for many years, but we were no longer kind or thoughtful toward each other.

I left my husband after forty years of marriage and I know it was the right thing to do. Despite the fact that we had everything that should make you happy, I was dissatisfied and was searching for something. Jerry was not happy either. We had five grown children and four grandchildren, a big beautiful home, cars, horses, stable and all the money and prestige we had dreamed about when we were young. It wasn't enough for me, however, as something inside was not being fulfilled and I was in turmoil.

Jerry James and I fell madly in love in college and we were married on the day we graduated from Wake Forest University in Winston-Salem, North Carolina. It was a stormy, passionate relationship from the beginning. We had attended a junior college together, where he was president of the student body and I was the vice-president. We began dating. He was a football player, good-looking in a masculine way and a nice young man. His mother, Alva James, who was a former missionary, was very much against our relationship from the start. She said I was from a family full of divorce and of course she was right, which I couldn't deny. It was obvious that she looked down on my family and I don't think she ever changed her mind about me.

Nevertheless, on June 6, 1960, we had a beautiful wedding with our families present, in the Reynolda Gardens, which is attached to Wake Forest. We went to Florida on our honeymoon and Jerry learned that he had been accepted at Stetson University Law School in St. Petersburg. Since I had majored in sociology, I was able to secure a position at the Florida Department of Welfare while we were there. The plan was for both of us to return to Florida in September and begin our life together. The universe, however, had other plans for me and Florida called within days of the honeymoon.

They informed me they were desperate and that I needed to begin my job as a social worker immediately. After being married only a few weeks, I drove with Momma to Daytona, where she met Iris for a vacation. I continued to St. Petersburg alone, which was difficult. Jerry remained in Winston-Salem, working in a tobacco factory in order to have money on which we would live until I got paid which took two months. The YWCA where I had planned to live for the summer no longer existed in St. Pete, so I rented a room with a wonderful lady whose husband was not with her, either. He was a truck driver and had been in a terrible accident earlier, in which he was badly burned and was now confined to a hospital in Minnesota. Their only income was the boarding house, so she had to stay and manage it. I lived there for three months, until Jerry came. She and I became good friends. She didn't drive; therefore I drove her to where she needed to go and in turn she did a great deal for me, such as laundry and cooking. This was a difficult time for us—Jerry and I, as well as my friend and her husband, who was alone in a hospital far away. Our friendship did make it easier and I will be eternally grateful for her companionship during that time.

Jerry and I reunited in the fall, when law school started. Prior to his arrival, I found an apartment close to the school so that he could walk each day, since my job required our only car. As a new, young social worker, I had far too many duties and responsibilities. I was a foster care worker: placing children in foster homes and appearing in juvenile court to make recommendations regarding their future, including severing parental rights of abused or abandoned kids. I also placed seniors in nursing homes, supervised the foster homes and did adoptions as well. I have wondered why in heaven's name an inexperienced person of twenty-two could have taken on the responsibility of making such vital decisions about people's lives. Of course, the salary was so low that no one with experience or one drop of good sense would have gone near that job. However, in my ignorance I liked it very much, although it was exhausting and I was on call 24/7. I did my best—yet I do wonder if I ruined people's lives. However, I was young and thought I could do anything. After all, the position did require it. Having gained a little wisdom, I now know that only someone who is desperate and unknowing would consider taking on all that responsibility at any age. Thankfully these responsibilities are divided up among several social workers now in the state's welfare system.

After two years I became pregnant, which upset Jerry. He felt I had tricked him into getting pregnant after we had agreed not to have a child until he'd finished law school. I did very much want to have a baby, but I don't remember tricking him. He was always aware when I was not on birth control. Rob Roy, a beautiful, healthy boy, was born in June 1962, after Jerry's second year in law school. Jerry was a proud father. I worked until early June, when he finished the year, at which time he returned to Winston-Salem, to his previous job since we had no other income. In those days, most businesses in Florida closed down in the summertime, especially in St. Petersburg where the retirees rushed to cooler climates when hot, muggy weather descended heavily upon Florida.

Momma came to stay with me in a home where I was house-sitting for an elderly couple since Jerry and I needed to save the rent money. She nearly drove me crazy, constantly asking if I was in labor and reminding me she'd had all her babies quite easily at home. She seemed to think I could too, and that I should go into labor, drop that baby right then and there and get it over with. She wanted to go home for many reasons, but primarily because she wanted to sleep in her own bed, of which she informed me at least every hour. She was thrilled when Rob was born and, to my surprise, she always told him how proud she was to have been there when he came into the world. They were always close, and she simply chose to forget our long, hot and almost miserable summer together in St. Pete. Momma always remembered what she wanted to remember, the way she wanted it to be. Maybe that's a good thing.

Rob was born on Father's Day, and when he was a week old, we flew to North Carolina—only to learn that Jerry had hepatitis and was living at his mother's home. According to his mother, the baby and I were not to come near him, or we would get sick too. I called the doctor, who said if we both got a shot of gamma globulin we would be perfectly safe. After we got the shots and arrived at the house, she was not happy and informed me I would have to sleep in the guest bedroom, away from

Jerry. She had recently lost Jerry's father and was therefore a little more possessive than usual regarding her son.

With the doctor's permission, I moved into Jerry's room ... but I lived to regret it. She had many ways to show her disapproval of my every action. I have come to believe, she did not want anyone, especially us, having sex in her house. Five years later, when I became pregnant with the twins (my fourth and fifth child), she gave me a book titled *Sin, Sex and Self-Control*, and it wasn't meant for her son. Jerry said, "Well, Mom, two out of three ain't bad. We have sin and sex down right."

During our stay in her home, she corrected everything I did for Jerry, letting me know he had been her son much longer than my husband and she knew what was best for him. She also had become extremely frugal, especially about food, and served leftovers until every morsel was eaten or it became moldy. We would sneak out to get hamburgers— or anything—which was always better than what we had in the house. Considering the food, the situation between his mother and his wife, lack of privacy and very little sex, it was not a pleasant place for Jerry, either.

He soon suggested we go home early to Florida, and we arranged to return to our previous apartment. His mother insisted we buy a car belonging to his brother, Larry, who had gone into the Peace Corps. We could not afford the payments, but she played the guilt card on Jerry and he caved in and we took it. I went back to work as soon as we returned in July, while he recuperated and watched the baby. He returned to law school in September. His parents paid his tuition and I paid the other bills. He worked as a motel night clerk, where I would drive him after classes, pick up the baby, and then I'd return for him late at night. I must admit it was a good thing we had that dependable car with all that driving with a baby on board. I also used it in my job. The schedule was hard on both of us, yet we knew it was necessary in preparation for the life which we were determined to make for ourselves.

Jerry graduated with very good grades and secured a job with an older attorney in East Florida, while waiting to see if he'd passed the bar exam. However, we had just gotten settled into a little house which belonged to the attorney and his wife, when her behavior became odd. She was obviously fearful that Jerry would take her husband's clients and, as office manager, she made it known that she was not happy he was there. She wouldn't allow him to answer the phone, even while they were on vacation. There were other signs that she was insecure with another attorney in the office. This was difficult to believe, considering that Jerry had not passed the bar yet and her husband had hired him. He also was past sixty-five and had said he wanted to retire. People are often unpredictable, and this was a lesson in how odd someone can behave, even when they are supposed to be normal.

When the couple told Jerry they were letting him go, it was an absolute shock for both of us. Jerry and I had decided that social work was too exhausting for me as a new mother. Therefore, I had taken the Florida State teachers' exam and accepted a teaching position. I'd never had an education course in college, but they had given me a teacher's manual, a classroom packed with students and a huge set of books—although I had no idea how to begin to teach those students. Everyone promised me that I would have help, but no one offered any assistance except to say, "Honey, don't worry, I know you'll do all right with those kids." This wasn't at all comforting, and I was frightened that those fourth-graders' education would be ruined, which would ultimately lead to lifelong failure for all thirty-four of them.

On finding out that Jerry had lost his job, I panicked. I was again the breadwinner in the family, in a profession where they would soon learn that I was incapable of performing even up to middling level. I simply wanted to bolt and run and I secretly made plans to do so. In the three previous years, I had graduated from college, married, moved at least six times, went alone to Florida, started a new and exhausting job with children's lives in my hands, found an apartment, plus I had supported us for three years. Also, I had a baby without Jerry in attendance (with

Momma bugging me), moved back to North Carolina for a month, fought off his mother and returned to my job early. Then, caring for a baby, I moved with Jerry to another town, took a state exam and accepted a teacher's job without knowing how to teach. I was now living in sheer terror at the thought of facing all those children who required five or six courses delivered to them per day for eight months.

I knew in my heart I was justified in running from it all. Not only was Jerry without a job, but we were soon to be evicted from the house which the attorney owned. I was far beyond exhaustion and unprepared for my job. I saw this as my chance to escape and allow a well-trained teacher to take over the class and save those kids. I knew I had been given this chance by a merciful God, to be saved from trashing the lives of innocent children.

To say the least, Jerry did not see it that way; he felt he was being abandoned in the worst of times. He had not had an easy time of it either, but I told him I was going to North Carolina with the baby, and to call me when he had a job and a house for us. Jerry was beside himself at my possible desertion and begged me not to go, reminding me we were supposed to be together in this. He couldn't understand my fear, and I think he never forgave me for thinking of leaving him at that miserable time. I can't blame him, though I can still feel my almost blinding need to escape. I managed, somehow, to head for that classroom despite an overwhelming urge to pick up my baby and run like crazy.

Jerry began looking for a job in nearby Ft. Pierce, while I started studying the schoolbooks as if my life depended on it. By then, I could see that nothing was going to rescue me or those unfortunate kids from that doomed classroom.

Believe it or not, I loved teaching and my thirty-four students survived the year quite well. I even received a good recommendation when I moved to another school. Again, I wonder why a school system would give an inexperienced woman in her twenties with a sociology degree, all those students to educate?". It was obviously because of the ridiculous salary and the heavy responsibilities that others wouldn't take the job. We talk about how important our children are, but this country has not yet put education as a priority nor do we pay educators as professionals.

Jerry soon found a job paying thirty-five dollars a week, which was the going rate for a lawyer who hadn't heard from his bar exam. In October, he finally received word that he had passed the bar. His salary went up; however, the money never seemed to get any better, as there was a catch to his "raise." This attorney's wife also ran his office and she made life difficult for Jerry. The agreement was that he would be paid a small percentage for the work he did on the attorney's cases and slightly higher for any cases he brought into the office. Since he did not know anyone, he didn't bring in many cases for a long time, and when he did, she would declare them her husband's client for one reason or another.

As soon as possible, Jerry opened his own office in the same town. By the time Rob was six years old, we had five children, including two more boys and twin girls. The girls were one year old when he opened his law office in 1969, and I'll never forget it—that was the day Neil Armstrong walked on the moon. Once he had his own office, Jerry did exceptionally well. He never enjoyed ordinary legal work but was very successful as a real estate developer and businessman, becoming well-respected in this area of the law. Jerry always felt he had to prove his ability to his father, an attorney who evidently didn't think he was very capable. We were both ambitious, and he declared he was going to be a millionaire by the time he was thirty years old. He accomplished this in part through his law practice, but mostly through buying and selling Florida real estate, which he enjoyed immensely.

I had worked for several years when Jerry asked me to stay home permanently to care for the children. I resisted at first, when he said, "Stay home and I'll take care of you." I loved my job and suggested that he stay home and let me take care of him. That didn't go over very well. At that time, I had a position helping to develop a new department in the county schools. I also acted as a teacher and social worker with migrant children, coordinating the resources of the community to provide food, dental and health care for them. It was satisfying work, yet I decided it was wise for me to be at home and care for our children. Jerry definitely could make more than I would ever be able to earn in education, and the children needed me there for them. Eventually, we bought acreage outside of town and built a large ranch home and later a stable to house his horses. I cared for the children and was an avid volunteer in my community, organizing the volunteer program for the county school system, serving as president of the chamber of commerce and working to develop various community programs.

Jerry and I also were active in political campaigns and donated to various charities. I became a leader in our community and he could have been, if he had been interested in doing that, since he was highly respected in his profession and business. My main focus as a volunteer was for children. I spearheaded a campaign to establish a taxing district that provided funds for kids' programs. A ten-member council with decision-making powers decides how funds are disbursed and the council now has a multimillion-dollar budget for supporting programs for children within the county.

Also, I represented the League of Women Voters in state hearings, to oppose a nuclear power plant being built by one of the most powerful utility companies in the country on an island off the coast. The utility company took me to court, declaring that I was practicing law without a license, but the judge ruled I had a right as a citizen of the county to oppose the plant. Not surprisingly, we lost against one of the richest utilities in the country, who brought in experts from all over the country.

We gave them a good fight. Later, a utility company executive told us that "No other nuclear plants have been built in the U.S. since our fight because of people like you opposing them." We thanked him graciously, although it certainly was not meant as a compliment. We believe that there are safe, cheap and nondepletable sources of energy which could be developed. And these do not produce radioactive waste products.

Jerry and I raised five children together, but he and his brother, Larry, were mistreated by his dad and he did not have a good role-model as a father, nor did I. I always felt he was much too hard on the children—like his dad had been to him - and Jerry felt I was too soft. Admittedly, I was like my Momma, so I wasn't a very nurturing mother either, although my children knew I loved them. Jerry and I were always there for them, but we argued a great deal. We had some problems from the beginning: two strong egos, constantly clashing. Jerry tried to control me through our money, but this didn't work. I usually found a way to do whatever I wanted, which upset him. Because of my experience with my father, I also had a deep-seated distrust of men and it was a constant game of one-upmanship between us. This naturally was not good for the children and affected them. He and I had completely different interests; he loved his horses and I did not, I loved to travel and he didn't. Jerry preferred that I stay at home, but I loved traveling all over the world with the children or my Mom.

As we got older and the children were gone, we grew even further apart. After forty years together, I knew he was not happy and I definitely was not. I had almost made my decision to leave, but when he was diagnosed with cancer, I stayed for a year to be with him through the chemo and surgery. Soon after hearing the doctor say he was free of cancer, I told him I was leaving. He was shocked, and later said he thought my leaving took courage and that he wouldn't have been able to leave. I had thought our relationship might improve during his illness, but it didn't, so I assumed he wanted out too.

I left my lovely home and thirty acres with a creek, ponds and thick Florida woods, which we had worked many hours to beautify. I loved our place and during the approximately twenty years at the ranch, we shared our home, the land and horses with the community. We held many charitable events there, especially with kids who loved the horses as well as the freedom to run and play on the open land. I knew, however, that leaving all of this was necessary for both of us if we were to be happy. By then, I had taken a self-development course and had decided I could be happy by using the tools that the course provided me. I also knew I had never been really happy in my entire life, which I could not blame on Jerry.

In 1999, I began a course called Avatar® by author Harry Palmer and it actually changed my life; I was able to release a lot of unhappiness and pain from my past. I began to write poetry and to focus on my own deliberate spiritual journey. Jerry was not impressed and thought Avatar was just an emotional crutch. He resisted feeling negative emotions resulting from childhood and had not yet forgiven his father for his cruelty or for his brother's severe mental problems. It seemed he found it painful to delve too deeply into his emotions at that time. I had decided to deal with my feelings about my unstable, confusing childhood and to become a more openly loving person, especially with my children. With my new goal, we grew further apart and we had less in common than ever. It was extremely difficult to leave my home and my life, which contained the wealth and security I had always wanted. I was determined, though, to let go of my deeply painful memories and to be happy. I drove away from what might be called a mansion, while pulling a fifteen-foot trailer- smaller than my bedroom.

Momma questioned my sanity and was sure I was giving up the financial security she had longed for all her life and that she wanted for me. In response to her concern, I told Momma I had learned one thing for certain: "You can be miserable in a mansion and happy in a small trailer." Momma eventually accepted my divorce after she felt I would continue to be financially secure.

I loved Jerry for many years and that love has changed, yet still exists in a different way. The family, at this point, is coming together, and I envision us even more loving and supportive of each other one day.

Before I left the marriage, I set the intention that I would make the financial settlement and the divorce as easy as possible and there would be no bitterness on my part. This intention has been valuable in making everything easier, with less drama. I tried to remember through the rough times to trust and know that all would work out well. Our son, Scott had said to me he was fearful that when I hired a lawyer, the divorce would turn nasty. I promised I wouldn't use one and would know I could trust Jerry. Some of my family were not sure that was wise. Still, I didn't use a lawyer. Jerry was fair, for, although he is not known to part easily with his money, he gave me what I wanted. I knew everything we owned since he had insisted, when he was ill, that I document all our assets in case of his death. Therefore, I had a record of our money and property, which was around one million dollars. Our children have always believed Jerry wanted to know that I was secure financially, and I respect him for it. I appreciate that he was fair, and we have slowly become friends in the years since we separated. I'm sure that will continue.

One day prior to leaving, I stood on the bridge that my son Rob built across the lovely stream on our property and said farewell. I said goodbye to my home, my husband and a full life there, and then looked to the future. I wrote a poem titled "Goodbye, My Love," into which I invested much of my pain on leaving. That was tremendously helpful through the heartbreak involved in separating myself from Jerry and the life we had built together. I promised myself never to have regrets about leaving and not to become bitter. I could have been a better wife and he could have been a better husband; yet I know I did the right thing for both of us and I have never wanted to return.

I do admit that in the first few months I wanted him to ask me to return just so I could say "Absolutely not!" He never did, and I should have known it was not going to happen. This seems strange now, from my present point of view, but I imagine that many others who have left a relationship have had that same stupid fantasy. I think I wanted to know he was suffering too. I'm sure he was; we were important to each other for a very long time.

The divorce was difficult for all five of our children, although they were each over thirty years old. I understand now, no matter what age children are when parents' divorce, it is difficult for them to come to terms with it and not to take sides.

I try not to blame Jerry more than myself because in my heart I know we were both responsible. I do feel he was too controlling and I was not pleasant to live with at that time. I could have been less argumentative and more accommodating, but it was not in my nature then. He respected me in many ways, but never liked for me to disagree with him, which maybe I did too often. He always felt I put the children before him- and perhaps I did, but I felt he was jealous of them.

We especially disagreed on raising the children and about money. He was a conservative and I was a liberal, he was a Republican and I was a Democrat. He prepared for "the worst-case scenario" and I tended to expect only good (neither of which was reasonable). We literally began to look at the world with opposing philosophies. He would also remind me that he was the one who made the money and he would therefore be the one to control it. I told him that if we divorced, I would be awarded one-half of the money and assets, but he did not accept that. We were on a collision course as two people who had changed drastically during the years since we had met as nineteen-year-old college students. He was happy staying at home in the stable with the horses, which were his passion and of course I wanted more.

As I got older, I became even more independent. I wanted to go places, try new things and find new challenges, but he preferred home and wanted me there too. I had obtained my Master of Science in Human Resources when I was about fifty-seven and wanted to begin studying for a doctorate, but he refused to pay for it. It was time for me to move on, or we could have begun to hate each other, and I didn't want that. Perhaps neither one of us was "wrong," or both of us were, but the truth is that we no longer brought happiness to each other.

Jerry and I loved each other and had a very passionate relationship in all aspects for many years. From beginning to the end, it was volatile; Jerry had a terrible temper and I was good at firing back. We were each afraid to surrender to love, for we both were unable to trust and were fearful of losing control because of our painful childhoods. I was no longer in love, even though I cared for him, but we were not being thoughtful or kind to each other. I do know that leaving, despite the difficulty, was best for both of us. We did have many good times, and I will always be thankful to him for everything he has contributed to my life. This includes our five children, living in the lap of luxury and having a relationship with a man who is intelligent, charming and fascinating in many ways.

I began to yearn for the peace of mind and happiness that I was unable to find in the relationship. I'm sure Jerry has his own ideas as to why the marriage failed and perhaps he will tell his side one day. He taught me a great deal and I will always love him in a way, for love can turn into friendship if you do not allow it to turn into hate. He holds a special place in my heart as the man with whom I was truly in love for many years. He contributed tremendously to my life and it was with him that I reached most of my childhood dreams. I believe that in time, he will be able to say that of me as well, for our life together was very interesting and productive too.

Many great philosophers have said we choose our life and I wanted to do that, and I set about doing it. I decided I wanted to be a different and better person than I was, and I've transformed my life. I am, however, still working toward becoming the best mother, grandmother, sister and person that I can be. As someone has said, "I'm better than I was, but not as good as I plan to be." I know I am happier and more peaceful than I have ever been, and I believe that is probably the most important thing in life. This happiness took a lot of forgiveness for others and for myself before I was able to find peace. I sincerely want every member of my family to forgive all, learn to love themselves and to find the happiness this can bring. Everyone deserves to be happy.

# Goodbye, My Love

I love you deep in my heart, but I must say goodbye
I feel like my heart will break, but I will say goodbye.
Do not become bitter, do not wither up and die
We really can be happy, we can hold our heads high.
So, hold your charm and keep your shining facade
But maybe we'll be happy if we don't try so hard.
Do keep growing, stay handsome as I go my way
How I shall miss all of you, when I go far away.

You gave me love and joy and shelter many times
I did love being there in the shower of your kind
You're my first real home away from all that I knew
You will forever be that, whatever in my life is new.
May we never lose our good memories of this place
No matter how we are running in that other race.
I must leave now, and make a life in another place
Always know this, that nothing can ever you replace.
So let us say goodbye, and remember our sweet love
For it was strong and good and it came from above.

# Forgive Me

I must forgive myself
First for
My childish sins
My daughterly lack
My sisterly pains
My wifely transgressions
My motherly mistakes
Yes
I forgive myself
Of all
And lovingly accept
Me
As my magnificent self
So I can love all other
Magnificent souls.

# Our

# Brazilian Friend,

# Luiz

Luiz brought much love into our lives and taught us how to be better people.

This book would not be complete without telling you about the most amazing person I have ever known—our Brazilian friend, Luiz da Silva. His story is truly one of great courage. His grandfather was a slave in Brazil, Luiz had eleven brothers and sisters and he and his family lived in dire poverty as he grew up in rural Brazil. Luiz now has several degrees, including his Doctorate of English, and without a doubt it took great ability plus unbelievable determination to accomplish what he has.

Luiz did all this and at the same time has been a gentle, caring person, while gaining many friends along the way. That is a very unusual ability, for most ambitious people are totally focused on their goals and often leave family and friends behind. Luiz now has three sons and these handsome young men have each graduated from a university in the United States. Luiz's wife and the mother of his sons is a beautiful Brazilian lady, Celia', who is an attorney. They love to travel and they have friends all over the world.

Luiz's story is extraordinary and one which is an example for all: of an ambitious poor boy from the lower class of Brazil, who wanted to transform his life. He was determined to get the best possible education, yet was always thoughtful and considerate to everyone during his quest to succeed. Luiz, as a man of color, had many obstacles to overcome in his country and in this country as well. He knew he would have the opportunity to earn more as a teacher with an American university degree. It was not an easy road; he never gave up, although it took him many years to get the education he wanted. Luiz paid his dues because he never expected charity; he works hard and is responsible. He is also able to charm everyone with his sincere kindness, his humility and his willingness to do whatever it takes to attain his goal. This is how he has been able to achieve so much in life.

We first met Luiz when he came to the States with a group of Brazilians who were here for a short stint as exchange students. I'm not sure how we were fortunate enough to get the best of the group, but I shall always thank God that Luiz came to us. He was young and unmarried at the time, and it was obvious he was the leader of the students by the time they arrived in Florida. During the weeks the students were here, he also won the hearts of the other host families, for he was courteous and spoke English better than the others. Even here in the South, Luiz became the favorite, although the other students were more sophisticated. He was irrepressibly positive as well as thoughtful, and it was obvious to all that he would succeed at whatever he attempted in life.

Before the end of their stay as exchange students, Luiz approached us to ask if my husband and I would be willing to sign for him to return to the States to earn a degree at an American university. We did not need to put up any funds—only sign a document, an affidavit of support, that we would if it should ever become necessary. Naturally, Jerry was reluctant because we had only known Luiz for a matter of weeks. I knew, however, that this was the perfect opportunity for me to "pay it forward." I had promised the gentleman who had assisted me while in college to help others, and Luiz appeared as my perfect candidate. My husband and I discussed it further, realizing we were moving into unknown territory, taking in someone we didn't really know and could lose money if anything negative should occur. I was determined we'd back Luiz because I knew he deserved a chance for a better life than he was able to achieve in Brazil. Jerry and I made the decision to move ahead and it turned out to be an exciting adventure which has been very rewarding.

Right after Luiz came to stay with us, he attended a kindergarten play that Jody and Abby were in. When it was over the two girls came running to us and hugged Luiz who they already loved. One of the children said to them, "Why do you have a black man living in your house". Quickly both girls responded, "He is not black, he's Brazilian!"

Luiz came in 1974 and stayed for about ten years. He did not live with us all of this time and eventually moved to Gainesville to attend the University of Florida. Despite the fact that he had a college degree from Brazil, he knew an American university degree was important. He worked hard and finally graduated from the University of Florida in 1979. He always remained in touch with us, and we supported him in other ways—yet never had to actually put up money, that I can remember. All those years he worked for us or others, tirelessly, with that steely determination that you rarely see in a young man. He made many other friends and joined a Christian church, which he loved, with a lady who had become like a mother to him. Luiz's mother and father were older when he was born, and died while he was young. His older brother had acted as his substitute father and Luiz needed a mother figure. I don't know if he realized that I was jealous of her, but I knew she was a wonderful addition to his life and important to him.

While here, Luiz's friend, Hans, and his father visited him from Austria for a week or so. I loaned my condominium on the ocean to them and, in return, Hans and Luiz served Jerry and me, plus six of our close friends, a delicious dinner in our home. This was a seven-course gourmet dinner with the works. Hans, a French-trained chef, cooked a fabulous meal and Luiz served the dinner as a sophisticated waiter with the proper waiter's uniform, including the requisite small white towel across the arm. They provided the flowers, wine and candles, as well as the food. It was a delightful evening with good friends, good food and great fun with our perfect dinner staff. That dinner for eight may have been more expensive than it would have been for them to stay at a hotel. Even so, I shall never forget that special evening and their thoughtfulness.

Luiz made our life better because he is an unselfish person who really likes people. We provided him with opportunity and some material things, and we never lost any money. He contributed more important things to our life: respect, caring, thoughtfulness—and he gave our children unconditional love. I believe Luiz gave my children more loving attention than perhaps we were giving them at the time, since issues, work and life in general were taking too much of our time. I am very grateful to him, and my children still have wonderful memories of time with Luiz, especially in the old Beetle Volkswagen Jerry bought for him. He has been a blessing to our family, especially for our children, and each has written about some of their memories with him.

Rob: He relates that he was going through his tough teenager, cowboy stage most of Luiz's time with us, but even then he realized that this man was a good human being who contributed much to our family.

Scott: Luiz's first day with us all five kids were swarming around him like he was from another planet. We wanted him to speak Portuguese. Rob asked him how his name would sound and he said, "Hob." He pronounced my name "Escot," and we all laughed. We loved it and we have all loved him ever since.

Bo: I can never forget the wonderful times that we had with Luiz, especially in "Herbie," the VW Beetle which he named after the car in the Disney movie, *The Love Bug*. Our entire group would crowd into the little car, and Luiz would laugh and holler, "Go, Herbie, go!" Then we'd all join in with: "Go, Herbie, go!" -happily encouraging the car to move forward. Then off we'd go for a great day of fun and games with Luiz.

Abby: I remember when we saw "Herbie" pull up, we raced outside to welcome our Brazilian friend. As he hugged and greeted us, he'd often let out a larger-than-life laugh. Even today, over forty years later, I remember the sound of his joyfully, distinctive laugh and it still makes my heart smile. Whether he was taking us in "Herbie" to the local Dairy Queen for a hot fudge sundae, yelling out the name "Pelé!" as he showed us how to score a soccer goal, or swimming laps in the pool while my twin sister and I hung on to him, Luiz knew how to stir up fun with big laughs and create childhood memories that last a lifetime.

Jody: Luiz came into our lives at a time the five of us needed lots of attention. With parents who were working toward success goals, there was only so much attention they could manage. We were a five-pack of rocket fuel energy and growth hormones. Luiz stepped in, young and happy. He'd already had a lifetime's worth of hard work in Brazil and was determined to make a life better than his own parents could have ever imagined. He would do it through an American education and was willing to give all he had to care for this crazy, loud James Gang of aggressive kids in order to reach his dream.

Luiz returned to Brazil in 1983 for a visit, but was unable to get back into the United States because of a technical/monetary problem. He married, had three boys and was later able to return to earn his doctorate in 1997 from the University of Southern Mississippi. (Luiz dedicated his doctoral thesis to Jerry and me, as well as several others who had assisted him in the States.) All three of his sons now live in the States, two of whom have graduated from the University of Southern Mississippi. The other graduated from the University of Florida, married an American girl, became a citizen and has given him a beautiful granddaughter who he and Celia (and the two uncles) obviously adore. I suspect that his other sons may become citizens here too, since Luiz and Celia' love visiting. As I said, his story is amazing and I have barely touched on it, so I sincerely hope he will write a book about his journey. He was in his late twenties when he came to the States, so I can only imagine how he accomplished what he did in Brazil prior to that. I'd love to know more and it would be an inspiration for many people all over the world. I tell him often to start writing, and I hope our memories will get him started.

Luiz gave me the perfect opportunity to pay back what many people contributed in my determination to get an education and achieve my childhood dreams. I'm proud to have played a small part in his courageous journey, as I'm sure Jerry is too. I think of Luiz as the true Renaissance man because he has friends from many nations, plus he is interested in the world and its people. He is also a gentle man with a great deal of strength, who appears to be uncomplicated yet has great depth. Luiz brought much love into our lives and taught us how to be better people, contributing more to our family than we gave him. I am very grateful to him and will always consider him my friend.

# Beauty of Life

I am surrounded by
Beauty every day
I am offered the pure
Joy of life each day
I drink in the sky's bright
Awesome starry night
I bathe in the lovely Seas
Sit under the leafy trees
I Love every hour
Enjoying God's flowers
I wash in the sun's rays
Am filled with awe always
As I am surrounded by
Beauty each day.

Bo, Jody, Abby, Rob, Scott, Jerry and Judy

James Gang 1975

Bo James, Celia' and Luiz Da Silva (our Brazilian
Student) Judy and Jody James 2016

# Filling

# My

# Soul

One day while driving 80 miles an hour on the highway, I went inside a lovely rainbow teeming with color.

I have been on a spiritual journey since the day I was born. Actually, every person is on their spiritual journey from birth—we just don't recognize it. We make decisions every day on how we will live our life and how we relate to the Divine. In 1999 when I was sixty-one years old, I took the self-development course, Avatar, to which my daughters, Abby and Jody, introduced me. This program teaches the tools necessary to examine your core beliefs and release the negative ones, giving us an ability to create our lives more deliberately. Four years later I found the spiritual philosophy/religion of Ernest Holmes, which is nondenominational and teaches that we are all the sons or daughters of God.

I had always felt the religion of my childhood was too restrictive and negative. My new spiritual philosophy is positive and teaches that God loves us unconditionally. It also assures us that we have unlimited potential as well as the responsibility to develop our potential to the highest level. We are made in the image of God and have all our Creator's characteristics, but on a smaller scale. The tools (from Avatar) to let go of my negative beliefs and my new spiritual religion go hand in hand since both are positive, and have been vitally important in bringing about a transformation in my life.

I knew I wanted to be a better person than the ambitious, "do whatever it takes to succeed" type of person I was, who sometimes hurt people's feelings in the process. I had justified what I did by believing that the things I wanted to accomplish were good for the community. My motives, however, were not always the best, but I was sincere in trying to make improvements in my community, particularly for disadvantaged kids. I also wanted the public recognition of accomplishing my goals and I thought I knew what was right. This was in the 1960s, '70s and '80s, and women were held back, so I felt challenged to prove we were as intelligent and capable as men (or maybe even more so). I therefore became president of many organizations, including the local male-dominated Chamber of Commerce. As a community leader, I won various awards in the process and, although I was honest, it was obvious that my ego was front and center. All of this didn't satisfy the yearning for something more, which was like a thirst that came from deep within.

I later realized I was doggedly playing out my Momma's plan for me to be an achiever and do what she didn't have the opportunity to accomplish as a child of the Great Depression. I didn't really know myself, so I was singing her tune, and at some point I realized it was her song and it wasn't right for me. I simply was not happy. I'm not blaming that on Momma, because I made my own choices. The fact is she told me I should be an achiever, and I thought, *Boy, that's for me!* I took it on wholeheartedly. Admittedly, I was desperately working for Momma's approval because I felt that no matter what I did, it was never good enough for her. That may sound as if I'm trying to justify my behavior, but I deliberately chose that role for myself when I could have rejected it. I knew, too, that it would assist me in moving up the social ladder and that was one of my major goals.

I discovered early in my soul-searching that in attempting to "save all the children," I was desperately trying to save myself as a child. This was a mind-blowing realization, knowing I had created a burden for myself and was carrying this heavy monkey on my back. This motivated my work for children and caused the dark emotions which were always present. During an Avatar exercise, I symbolically lifted that "monkey" off and laid it down under a big oak tree in Sarasota. I swore never to pick it up again. It was a tremendous relief to realize I didn't have to save all the children in the world who might be suffering as I had in childhood. Not only did I not have to save them, I could not. Happily, I accepted the idea that providing support through good organizations that are experts, assisting one child at a time and positive prayer would be the best way to make an impact regarding children.

I began to understand that being a happy, loving person who is at peace within is what's truly important and that became my goal. By gaining an appreciation for what I had accomplished as a volunteer in schools, in health care and after-school programs, I was able to forgive myself for my pushy, know-it-all behavior. I learned to be a feminist without being aggressive, yet remaining determined, and by being a better role model. I accepted that you can attract more with a honey personality than with a too aggressive attitude. I came to appreciate my achievement for the Children's Services Council that still provides tax dollars to fund programs for hundreds of kids. Through my spiritual work, the persistent feeling of never being good enough also began to disappear as I learned to love myself. I sincerely believe that loving ourselves comes through learning to forgive ourselves and all who we feel may have wronged us.

Because of my childhood mobility, change continued to play a big part in my life. My siblings and I were transplanted so many times, our roots were as shallow as those of the tree whose roots run on top of the ground. Our real family roots in North Carolina had been painfully cut and bled a long time after Grandma turned us out. Moving about twenty times before finishing college prepared me for life's changes and caused me to invite it, but I do need a home as an anchor. I have always been curious and new ideas and challenges have made life more interesting.

I've been a lifelong student, receiving my masters' degree at age fifty-seven, and have continually taken classes ranging from computer science to spiritual courses. I'm fortunate to have had wonderful teachers, from high school to more recent spiritual teachers at the Center for Spiritual Living in St. Augustine. Many people have supported and taught me a great deal, which is especially true of my five children and Momma. Daddy taught me many lessons as well, but his always came with a boat-load of suffering. Still, I accept now, how really valuable they were.

My search for peace began about twenty years ago, and my life and my personality have been in constant transition ever since. I've always had a deep urge to develop spiritually and have had a need to dig deeper into the meaning of life. I truly believe, now, that my primary purpose on earth is to be happy by giving and receiving love because God is Love. I know the problems that show up in life are not problems unless I make them a problem by reacting, rather than accepting each as an opportunity to learn. I may not be able to control everything in my life, but I do determine how I react to what comes my way. For me, this means my happiness depends on how I look at life, and so I choose to be happy, to learn and evolve constantly.

There are seven billion people on earth who could keep the Creator busy, but I believe that God set the laws of attraction into motion and allows us to attract all that we deserve into our lives through gratitude and prayer. Thankfully, our Creator sent us guardian angels so we would have a little assistance surviving and even enjoying this complicated earthly life we have chosen.

I now have an ability to adjust to whatever comes my way because of my early experiences. Late in life, when it became necessary to begin a new and difficult journey, I was able to move forward. After leaving my marriage, I lived in North Carolina in the beautiful Blue Ridge Mountains for a few years, which was a period of reflection and healing. In the ten years after I left Jerry, I got a divorce, watched the 9/11 disaster, helped care for Momma until she passed away, bought and sold two houses and moved six times. Eventually, my children asked me to return to Florida, so I moved to the unique town of St. Augustine, which I have always loved. Those were difficult years, yet I became a new person—with the support of family, Avatar courses, a new spiritual philosophy, as well as a completely new and happier view on life.

Trust, which Momma taught me, plays a big part in my life. Momma often said, "Don't worry, 'cause 80 percent of what you worry about won't even happen, and the 20 percent will turn out alright in the end." Sometimes it seemed the end would never come but it did always work out. Momma was a true believer, and I learned that early, from a woman who had little reason to trust, yet who trusted to the end. This helped her accomplish a great deal in our lives despite very few resources. She inspired us, motivated us and taught us many good lessons for life.

The main thing I have learned in this life is that love is the most powerful force in the world and that we need to love ourselves first to sincerely love others. Holmes' spiritual philosophy teaches forgiveness, so I had to forgive all who I thought had hurt me, and especially myself. I felt I had been a lousy mother and this guilt stuck to me like black ink on white silk, which I feared could never be washed away. It has taken me longer to forgive myself for not being a nurturing mom than forgiving everyone else put together.

I assumed I was the worst mother on earth and that I had caused my children so much pain they wouldn't forgive me. Relieving myself of this guilt-laden idea was not as easy as laying that other burden down under a tree. My son, Rob is sure that we get the parents we need and says that his parents were perfect for him to develop on his spiritual journey. Each of my five children is a genius in their own way, and I enjoy being friends with them, now. I feel they have forgiven me most of my many transgressions as a mom. They are all a strong support system for me and I strive to always be there for them.

I'm still working on forgiving myself daily and have learned to love myself, which is the most precious gift you can possibly give yourself. I would say that God forgave me too, but I don't believe the Creator ever judges us; rather God sees us as perfection and loves us unconditionally. I've felt different from those around me all of my life. I have now learned to accept my uniqueness and to fully appreciate it by finding my own voice and expressing it. I had always loved poetry and wanted to write, but thought I wasn't the least bit creative. Immediately after my original Avatar course, I dreamed my first poem and, now, writing poetry is one of the delights of my life. I know I write poetry with the help of the Devine and often receive a poem almost complete, especially during meditation. I plan to publish several complete books of poetry.

In every place that I lived as a child, I tried to be the best I could and worked hard so as not to be a burden. I was treated well by the people who were forced to care for me, but still it wasn't easy. Many of them were not well-off and having an extra mouth to feed was a problem. I remember that most of my relatives were simply trying to survive and they had forgotten how to smile. The orphanage was the most unpleasant place. And adding to that was the horror of the murders along with a bitter housemother who didn't like her place in this world and was afraid to search for another. It's a miracle that although I was dropped off in many places- and some were bad- I was never abused or mistreated. I was often sad, yet I refused to become a victim, and appeared to be strong although I may not have always felt as brave as I pretended to be.

I was fortunate to have spent that full year as a seven-year-old, happy and secure in a foster home in the Blue Ridge Mountains. I will forever be grateful for that time, that place and the sweet, strong foster mother who nurtured me. Without a doubt, this time helped me to gain a strong sense of myself, along with the strength I needed to make it through some ugly times. I desperately needed this experience; it was the one place in my childhood that I truly felt wrapped in loving arms. I'm very thankful for all those who cared for me, fed me and kept me safe, even when they had few resources to share. Many of the Devines, who are Momma's family, often were there for us and I'm grateful to them, as well as the Webbs who gave us much affection.

I attend the Center for Spiritual Living in St. Augustine, which teaches the religious philosophy of Holmes and it has become a wonderful spiritual home. I know that everything I need is within, for the Divine resides in each of us, and that my life is shaped by my beliefs which I have the power to change. Change your thinking and you can change your life is a major principle in this spiritual philosophy. By releasing the pain of the past, I have chosen to be happy, which is why God created us. Meditation has been a major key in my transformation and has brought me tremendous peace of mind.

*Judy H James*

For the majority of my life I didn't like myself and didn't feel I was spiritual at all. I had always resented religion as represented by the many unhappy aunts and uncles and others in my childhood. The punitive God who would allow people to burn in hell for an eternity is not the divine God of love that I know. Mine is a loving presence that resides within, who has given us choice, wants our happiness and offers us time to get it right. I'm working on that and I'm better today than I used to be, but not as good as I want to be tomorrow.

From the beginning of the separation and divorce, my intention has been to become friends with my former husband and not to cause bitterness. I've tried never to speak negatively about Jerry, since we were together for more than forty years and I respect that time together. This has been helpful in my relationship with my children and satisfying in many ways. I know it was through our marriage that I was finally able to experience the life of luxury and to assist Momma to have a better life. It was a wonderful feeling to reach those goals in my life, although I came to know that money cannot make you happy. And neither can another person. You must find your own happiness and find it within, through a relationship with Spirit. My vision for my entire family is that each will fall in love with themselves, forgive all and find real happiness as we all become closer.

My purpose for this book has been to help my children, grandchildren and all my progeny to understand me and their extended family of the past. Someone once asked me: "How on earth did you turn out normal, considering your crazy life?" I'm not sure I'm normal but being open to new philosophies and accepting a God of love has helped bring me a new, wonderful vision of life. My Mom was open-minded too and liked new ideas, and I inherited these traits from her. All five of my children have contributed to my change in some way and they have been my best teachers, having always loved me even when they disagreed with me.

I know we are perfect just the way we are, but we can always get better and I believe we should give everyone an opportunity to prove themselves. Never judge anyone too quickly by their dress, their accent or their outer appearance. The worst may look and sound the best, but then again, the best may look and sound the worst. I believe if you judge quickly, you will be too easily fooled, and the one who does may turn out to be the fool. I have often been one by judging others too quickly. Listen, for all have something to say and a fascinating story to tell which has often surprised me more than I could imagine.

I have a very good life now, despite my challenging childhood, or perhaps because of it. I'd like to inspire children to realize they can have anything they really want if they believe in themselves and go for it. I know my challenges have made me more compassionate and understanding, and perhaps that is the true value of the painful experiences which come into our lives. Through many years and a whole lot of forgiveness, I've come to understand that both Daddy and Momma did the best they could. And even more important - they loved me better than they had been loved. My life has been an exciting ride and I wouldn't change it because it's been interesting and challenging.

My spiritual journey continues and there have been several stages of working toward happiness for me: first, being aware and facing the pain, then dealing with it through forgiveness; then accepting that my life's journey was exactly what it should have been and is perfect for me. God did not mistakenly drop me down in the wrong family, even though I was positive this might be true at one time. Another important process was to become aware of my thoughts and to think positive thoughts, especially about myself. We tend to put ourselves down, and as the old saying goes:" You can't believe everything you tell yourself or you will be miserable." Buddha, a wise and ancient man taught that it's more important to conquer our own minds than to conquer the world.

I've been privileged to have had several awesome spiritual experiences or epiphanies which have had a powerful effect on my life. My definition of an epiphany is an experience which is other-worldly, meaning not exactly explainable in this realm; and they have a profound effect on the person. My first one was rather dark—not bright and beautiful like the others—yet it led me to know I needed to begin my spiritual journey in earnest. It did not actually speak to me; nevertheless, I got the message loud and clear. Other epiphanies were beautiful experiences which helped me along my journey.

I had my first epiphany while at a retreat on Iona, a beautiful and serene island in the Hebrides, off Northern Scotland. They say the veil between heaven and earth is the thinnest on this little island, making it the perfect place to have an epiphany and other spiritual experiences. Soon after arriving, as I was about to go to sleep one evening, I went deep into a very dark place. There was an extremely black and almost overwhelming heaviness pulling me downward. Next, a huge sadness regarding my dad surrounded me, especially around my heart, and I realized it was his sadness and mine mixed together. In the beginning, it appeared that it was going to be a long, depressing time in the darkness, but it only lasted a matter of seconds.

When I came up and out of this depression, I had released the sadness and had forgiven myself, and him, for much of the unhappiness we had caused each other. It was an experience never to be forgotten. This was the beginning of understanding my dad and starting an emotional healing around him. Although I did not realize it at the time, it was the start of my true, deliberate spiritual quest and it was a powerful experience.

My next exceptional epiphany came when I asked the universe, "Do I have a guardian angel?" This was something I had always wanted to know and a wise lady named Carole advised me to ask and put it out into the universe. I was in the loveliest of places, in the early morning on green, rolling hills overlooking a mountain range called the Seven Sisters in my beautiful Blue Ridge Mountains when I silently asked the question. I was immediately immersed in an all-encompassing warmth from head to toe. A feeling of unconditional love came pouring over me like a warm, bright light. It is quite indescribable, for I had the feeling of a loving connection to something beyond this earthly realm. I always thought I had been watched over, but since then I have no doubt that God has sent me a guardian angel. This brings me a great deal of comfort and joy. I have also had several other less dramatic experiences that support my belief in guardian angels.

My third, fascinating epiphany was within a rainbow. I was driving home with a friend, Patrick (from Ireland), after attending an awesome Avatar course with approximately 3,000 people. We were all doing work in consciousness regarding taking responsibility for your life. On highway I-95, while driving 80 miles an hour, I went inside a lovely rainbow teeming with color and had an amazing experience. My friend and I saw the lovely rainbow up ahead and were admiring its vivid colors. Suddenly, I found myself inside the rainbow and was completely surrounded by a bright, warm haze of color. It reminded me of the beam that is made when the sun shines into a dark room, but it encompassed me completely in delightful specks of red. There was an absolute lack or feeling of reality, time or space—just total serenity. It was as if I were floating in a pool of love, with the sense of being totally at peace.

When I came back to my worldly reality of time and space, I discovered that I had continued to drive at a high speed. I wondered why I hadn't run off the road and killed us both. I wasn't at all disturbed by this thought, however, because I was blissfully happy and realized immediately that something was watching over me during that time. My friend and I discussed our amazing experience inside the rainbow, almost for confirmation, because neither of us was positive it was real. As we talked, we realized our experiences were quite similar, except that he was surrounded by the color purple and the warmth in my rainbow was bright red.

I have had other lesser, yet still important spiritual experiences and definitely hope to have many more. I have tremendous gratitude for these special times in my life and the delightful memories around them which continue to bring me joy. I want to hold on to those incredible feelings of bliss forever and often wish for another rainbow to engulf me. I trust there are many more blissful experiences in store for me.

Jesus changed the world by bringing us the greatest message ever - that of love. His message was to love God, love yourself and love your neighbor. Then he presented that revolutionary idea: love your enemy. To me this says that it does not matter what your enemy has done, you should have enough love in your heart to love them. The reason is - having that much love within us will assure that we will live in true prosperity because we'll be happy and have peace of mind. That is Jesus' truly wonderful message for the world and it brought a quantum leap in the world's consciousness.

I believe all good roads lead to God; therefore, we must find our own way and honor other religions as well. To believe that we are the only ones who've got it right is arrogance because one type of religion does not fit all seven billion diverse and brilliant human beings on this earth. We must find the religion that best suits us and accept that love is the most powerful force on earth, for God is love. I believe that Love heals all and can conquer all fear.

My hope is that my life story and experiences can be helpful to others, especially young people. I was born into poverty, and then for many years lived in wonderful prosperity. Now I know true abundance, which is knowing love, and maintaining peace of mind through my spiritual work. Ancient wisdom tells us that people who may appear to be rich, may actually be very poor; others may seem poor, but are very rich. For me, rich means having faith in the Divine, as well as appreciating the people and the beauty around me every moment and being grateful for it. That brings me happiness, for I believe it's impossible not to feel happy when you're being grateful.

The Golden Rule in one form or another is accepted by all major religions, and love is the only thing in life that is truly important.

I'm grateful for many things, especially those who have loved and supported me throughout my life including the angels that are always near. I know there is still much for me to do and experience before I leave this earth. And that is exciting.

At 62 years old, I had achieved the goals that I had dreamed of as a child. I had obtained a wonderful education, and my husband and I had more material things than most people in the world. As I had determined to do as a child, I was able to assist in making a better life for Momma, which gave me a great deal of satisfaction. As promised I had "paid it forward" by assisting others, particularly children. I was grateful and always felt the need to share our good fortune. Despite my success, I was not truly happy. I felt unfulfilled and decided to search for inner peace. Holmes teaches that when we decide to improve, the universe will deliver all which we need to accomplish our goal.

The universe delivered, and I began a deliberate transformation. With a new philosophy, wonderful support, and the tools to release negative beliefs, I discovered serenity. I found it through true forgiveness, opening-up to love, and serving others. I also achieved a deeper connection to my Creator by daily meditation.

My spiritual work fills and enlightens my soul as I continue my quest to become the best I can be. I now look forward to the many wonderous things I can create, plus all that which life has waiting for me to discover. My journey from tears to triumph has been a fascinating trip. I am extremely grateful. It has been full of amazing miracles leading to the peace and joy for which I was searching. I am also positive that this is available to all who truly seek it, as they search for a closer connection to the Divine.

# Rainbow's Gift

One sweet day the end of a rainbow
Came quietly down upon my path
I flowed through it ever so silently
As my body washed in color
My soul bathed in peace.
This wonderful gift is
Worth more than gold
For I was awash
In the promise
Of hope and
The light
Of God's
Love.

# Dancing

As I danced among the stars
I remember the sweet angels
Whispering in my ear
Remember dear one
The purpose on this
Your beautiful green earth
As throughout the universe
Is to live in pure joy
Smile often with delight
And love completely
As you are loved
For one day you'll return
To dance among the stars
Laugh with the angels
And dwell in the arms
Of Love forever.

# Surrounded by Love

I'm surrounded by Love
Given every day
As a heavenly wave
I'm surrounded by Love
In an earthly way
And
More loving each day
I'm surrounded by Love
And grateful this day
Surrounded by Love
A shower of affection
And
Each day perfection
I'm surrounded by Love
And all my beloved.

April 2018

# Epilogue
## Letter from Luiz DaSilva

Sao Paulo, August 8, 2018

My dear Judy:

How touching your saga has been! It moved me to tears as I avidly read page after page of your book. Also, I felt honored to have played a small part in it. Of course, I was just an accident in your beautiful trajectory to stardom. The reading also confirmed my appreciation for the magnolias that surrounded my dorm at the USM. You truly deserve the nickname of steel magnolia since you embody both the beauty of it and the humanitarian kindness that I have received in the South.

Now, 45 years later, I can appreciate even more your unselfishness in reaching out for me and lifting me from poverty to a new horizon in life. Despite not having known details of your upbringing, for I never wanted to pry into your privacy, I can understand that your life had not been as glamorous as I made myself belief it was. Yet, you were always tirelessly assisting me in more than one way, without any reproach or admonition. I remember that you could even "read" my thoughts in my early days in the Treasure Coast.

White Trash- Warm Hearts certainly instigated in me the desire to write a little about my wanderings and achievements. I may begin it soon. Many of my professional students were able to share part of the reading with me. They were amazed with all the praises you bestowed upon me. Are we talking about the same Brazilian person? I barely recognized me under the light. Nevertheless, I enjoyed reading about it and relived all the fantastic moments I had with your family and especially with the children. I vividly remember that once I went the girls' elementary school (show and tell session, I guess) and a student asked Jody why she had a black boy in her house and she replied: "Luiz is not black, he is Brazilian." I had been upgraded.

The life experience I have gained by being near you and your family has made me a better person and a more observant human being. We do share some of the difficulties but also some of the guts to move ahead. Luckily, my family was always united and I never felt neglected. However, my mother's behaviors sometimes surprised me too, especially when she would get mad and burn my school notebooks on the coal stove to stop me from going to school. Next morning, when she was calmer, I would sneak out of the house and resume my education.

Once again, I would like to congratulate you on your candid exposure of your life. The narrative is tender and inspiring to the people who are fortunate to read it, especially to our children who have been spared of the hardships of life. May God grant you the serenity you deserve and keep you as positive as ever. As the saying goes: There is nothing to stop a woman with determination.

Fondly,

Luiz DaSilva

Eternally grateful to you as my most valuable benefactor.

Judy James
St. Augustine, Florida
August 8, 2018

Luiz,

You truly have made those years I spent writing my book worth it. I cried the whole time I was reading your letter. You are not illiterate (which you mentioned earlier) in any way and I am so proud of you and thankful I played a small part in your life and your happiness. It thrills me that you are going to begin to write your story for it is the most amazing life-story that I have ever heard, and I am happy that my written journey inspired you to tell yours. Yours will inspire hundreds who are on a difficult journey of their own and give them hope. (So, do get to work, but I promise not to rush you since it took me 10 years to complete mine).

You married a lady who is beautiful both inside and out and now y'all have young sons (and a granddaughter) of whom I know you are proud and I feel much pride in them as well. I do hope you and Celia' can get to St. Augustine this Summer because I want to hug you both.

I also dream that you do become American citizens and I will assist that in any way that I can and will be there when they swear the two of you in as citizens. I am sure Jerry will assist too if you need him, so please let us know if we can help. In so many ways that would seem to be completing full circle what you started out to do. How wonderful that will be.

My Love always,

Judy

# About the Author

Judy James grew up poor in the Appalachian foothills. Her mother was forced to leave school in the sixth grade to work in the cotton mill and instilled in her daughter the belief that education was the gateway to escape the poverty, and the struggles of her youth. Desperate and determined, Judy walked up to the mill owner's mansion and courageously asked the stranger for a loan for college. When she promised to pay him back, he responded, "I'd rather you pay it forward and help others."

Little did he know that Judy had spent two years in a small mountain orphanage where two boys threw their lives away by murdering the principle and another boy. From this event, Judy's life was forever changed into someone hell-bent on helping children out of their suffering.

As Director of the Public-School Volunteer Program in a county filled with migrant children, she received numerous service awards and was honored as The Democratic Woman Of The Year for her advocacy for better after-school health and educational programs.

Later she spearheaded the establishment of the Children's Services Council which has raised millions of tax dollars that benefit single mothers and children in Florida. Given several leadership appointments by Florida governors, she advised other leaders on how to institute children's programs.

After forty years of leadership and service, this Steel Magnolia embarked upon a spiritual quest to connect with the divine and completely transformed her life. As a published poet and writer, she won Best

Short Story from the American Association of University Women of Florida.

She still has a very active life in a popular spiritual center in St. Augustine, Florida. She is a former board member and still serves as a spiritual counselor. Judy is loved and admired by her family and many friends for her fierce compassion and strong enthusiasm for life.